I0694280

A Million People, HADLEY

a novel by

Nick Macfie

A Million People, HADLEY

By Nick Macfie

ISBN-13: 978-988-82735-7-7

This book has been reset in 10pt Book Antiqua. Spellings and punctuations are left as in the original edition.

FICTION / Humorous

EB050

A Million People, Hadley was written during Nick Macfie's tenure as a *Reuters* journalist, but *Reuters* has not been involved with the content or tone of this book, which are the author's responsibility alone.

Published by Earnshaw Books Ltd (Hong Kong)

In memory of my father

Also by Nick Macfie
Hadley
Kiss Me, Hadley

CHAPTER ONE

A CHINESE TEENAGER wearing a yellow tee-shirt lay on his back in the middle of one of the busiest streets in Hong Kong, his arms and legs making a star and his trousers riding up his ankles. He was staring at a starry sky and not moving as someone round the corner played the sax like Kenny G, a tune at once baleful and dull. I heard raised voices. The music stopped. Someone shouted "fuck off" and something metallic skidded across the road.

There were two strange things about that night: one that the sky was starry and two that there was no traffic. Students had been protesting on the streets for three weeks demanding democracy. The police had used tear gas to try to break them up, here on Nathan Road, and then had helped them clean their eyes with bottles of water. Only in Hong Kong. Look, America: no guns. Look, Thailand: no bombs or snipers dressed in black hiding on rooftops. Look, China: no extra-judicial detentions with scores taken away in unmarked vans with darkened windows never to be seen again. No tanks and no soldiers. No blood of hundreds, if not thousands, seeping between the paving stones. Look: brilliant, alive Hong Kong.

"Hey, friend, have you seen my horn?" a man asked.

It *was* Kenny G, or someone that looked just like him. I examined the ringlets that fell flat and lifeless from the centre parting. I had had a few drinks. It could have been anyone.

"Your horn? No. I'm sorry."

"No sweat man. Everything's mellow."

"That's good."

"But some of these guys are unmellow." He flailed his arm in the direction of pockets of tired protesters, sitting or lying in the road between lines of tents, and a handful of police. I wasn't sure which guys he thought were unmellow. "I must be going," he said. "I'm looking for my instrument."

He dusted himself down for no apparent reason. Or had he had a fall? Had someone hit him? He headed north towards Jordan and stopped to talk to a group of students, presumably about his instrument. I didn't know and didn't care. I had come out of the pub to have a look at what was going on, to make sure everything was mellow in fact, and now I was heading back – a few blocks south and a long block east to Rick's Cafe, to be precise.

Everything was also unmellow at Rick's. There is something about my face, in bars in the early hours of the morning, that sometimes makes fellow expats want to beat the shit out of it. Until midnight, everything goes really well. And then the eyes turn towards me. The lawyers and the bankers and the hedge fund managers are somehow jump-started and hot-wired out of their drunken torpor, and they come at me, usually at a slight tilt, with a "why you…" and then lunge. They never get beyond "why you". It's not a question. It's a threat. But for me, it is a question. Why me? I've stood in front of the mirror trying to figure it out. Is it possible people mistake me for a miserable, sanctimonious prat? That's as close as I can get. I can't see the big picture. The wood for the trees.

I was drinking with a Christian missionary who was about four large gin and tonics ahead of me and pontificating about the protests.

"The students will never win anything," he said. "China will never budge on how the elections are run."

"I reckon they've already won," I said.

"Certainly China can never win without God on its side."

Oh lord. He started punctuating key points with little staccato pats on my knee. Fuck off. I stopped paying attention and he turned to some tourist on his other side.

At the far end of the basement bar, on the other side of the missionary, were three British lawyers and I could see the wood for the trees straight away. These three were pompous and corrupt and had long, effeminate moustaches which they rolled between their fingers like Plasticine. I was minding my own business, nursing a beer and not doing anything to annoy them as far as I could tell (they were at the other end of the bar, for heaven's sake!) It's possible I looked a little tired after a hard and long day, but that was all.

They were whispering between themselves now, their moustaches skipping up and down and in and out like flags. One of them broke away unsteadily and headed in my direction. He ran his hand along the bar to keep himself stable.

"What did you just call me?" he asked.

"I'm sorry?"

"What did you just call me? I heard you from over there."

"What did you hear?"

"You called me a cunt."

"No, I don't think so. Don't remember that."

And then it came. "Why you…" The prick was at my throat. What had I done? Maybe he could read my thoughts. "You bastard," he said. "You fucking bastard."

I was making an "aaargh" noise like a chain on a deck, staring at the ceiling, watching feeble Mexican hat-and-tortilla-shaped lights go round and round. I tried to peel his hands away, but he was in earnest. He was trying to kill me.

Then one of his mates – I swear this is true – leant over and asked me if I ever wondered why window panes, in temperate climates, didn't crack in the winter when it was hot inside and freezing outside. I looked at the man's eyes, at his mate's eyes, at the lights going round and round.

"Aaargh," I said.

"Don't you," the man went on. "Don't you worry about the integrity of the glass?"

The integrity of the glass. Do I worry about it? At two in the morning. With someone trying to kill me. Not really. The slippery lawyer released his grip and was dancing up the stairs and gone in seconds.

"Let that be a lesson to you," one of his mates shouted, another prat with a moustache.

He turned and headed for the stairs and that's where it got even more interesting. A woman in jeans, white tee-shirt and, for no good reason I could think of then, large, dark sunglasses was crossing his path to her table. What did the lawyer do? Stand back and let her pass? Apologise for being a prat? Apologise for his moustache? Not a bit of it. He raised his right arm and pushed her aside. So hard that she fell over a table, knocking people's drinks to the floor. And he didn't even turn back. He bounded up the stairs, his spindly bottom shaking between expensive worsted cotton. Another great night out for members of the bar in the heaving clubs of Hong Kong. Rick Astley was singing "It Would Take a Strong, Strong Man" on the sound system.

Customers were looking down at the woman but doing nothing to help. The Glaswegian manager was calling the bouncers to see if they could stop the lawyer at the top of the stairs fleeing into the hub-bub of the narrow, bustling Hart Lane (Hut Dut Dou in irresistible Cantonese), packed at that time of the morning with fey-looking gangsters, club girls with purple lipstick and tiny handbags, the occasional, sacked Western wannabe war correspondent and foolish lobster-coloured Englishmen in suits clutching briefcases and walking like crabs.

"My sunglasses," the woman said. "I've lost my sunglasses."

The customers were looking casually around for the glasses as I bent down to see if she was all right. I let my eyes stay on her face. The light was dim but I knew who she was and she knew

I knew.

"Are you all right?" I asked.

"I'm fine." She offered a quick, regal smile. "Just a little embarrassed. But that fellow. What a fucking dickhead."

Such eloquence. She was appealing for help. At least that's how I read it at the time after a handful of warehouse-strength gin and tonics, a couple of pints of Carlsberg and close to thirty cigarettes. In the tiniest fraction of a second, I noticed a man, probably South Asian, sitting at a table behind the woman and staring at me coldly. He was wearing sparkly ear rings.

"Would you like me to get you out of here?" I asked her. The question was loaded with inside knowledge, poignancy and integrity. She lifted and fluttered those famous big brown eyes. I took it for a yes. The customers were still looking for the sunglasses. "Come on then," I said. "Let's hit the boulevard."

Let's hit the boulevard? What? I helped lift her from the floor, holding her head to my shoulder and hiding her face. The not-entirely-lithe thirty-six-year-old body was warm and smelt of roses. I was, temporarily, the bodyguard. At the top of the stairs, I guided her left, heading for the car park opposite the Mariners' Club where I kept a twenty-year-old Mercedes. She put her left arm around my waist and buried her head in my chest.

Marina Makhdoom had her head in my chest, for fuck's sake. Marina Makhdoom, tipped by some who knew about these things to be prime minister of Pakistan one day, following in the footsteps of Benazir Bhutto, despite being a Christian in a Muslim-majority country. She was tipped to take over the mantle, as journalists liked to say. Not me. I didn't like to say that. I didn't know what a mantle was, except that Dracula had one. Couldn't be anything like a mantelpiece, that much I knew. It wouldn't make any sense. Marina Makhdoom was the daughter of a general who was being held under house arrest in Karachi without charge. He had been accused in various newspapers of plotting a coup against Bhutto's government back in the early nineties, of corruption involving an aerospace deal with France, of blasphemy and of colluding with the Taliban, who were seeking to install an Islamist state. And of course of being a closet Christian. I knew this much because I dealt with Pakistan stories on a daily, albeit shallow, basis. The government had refused to give a reason for holding him.

And for every unsubstantiated story about her father, there were five for his Western-educated younger daughter, most involving late-night parties, alcohol and affairs with unscripted men when she was married to the feted Colonel Usman Makhdoom, an army dental surgeon, no less, whose name sounded Scottish but wasn't. The latest story was that she had gone missing from the marital home in Lahore. But she got away with it, ironically, because she was a Christian. Some found her a fascinating side show, a peep show, and blamed all her depravity, if there was any, on her faith. Others thought she was a devil.

I had a story on my hands, anyway. I had *her* on my hands. What was I going to do? I mean, now we had hit the boulevard.

Makhdoom was not classically beautiful, but she had huge eyes that always looked like she had been crying. Wet was the word. She had huge, wet eyes which were always asking for attention. They invited you in. Literally. You could see yourself reflected elliptically in the brown irises (or dilated pupils) as you were talking to her. You were trapped like a goldfish in a bowl. I would find all this out later, but I thought it would be good to give a picture of her early in the piece. She was smallish and running ever so slightly to fat. But her skin was clear and kissable and her legs, as my dad would have said, were shapely. (But dad, that just means her legs have a shape! Fuck off, son) She had sensuous lips, glorious white teeth and dimples, low in the cheek, when she laughed. Mostly because of that, and her faith and the fact she never wore an all-enveloping veil, she received regular death threats from the Taliban and militant groups no one had heard of. She had as much chance of becoming prime minister as of being blown up. I knew little about her husband the colonel at the time except that he was much shorter than Marina, always travelled with a dozen bodyguards carrying big guns and once killed a man on a horse in a row about a goat. And that he once must have had ambitions in the dental field.

We reached my car. Marina stood up straight and looked at me.

"What do you think you are doing?" she asked.

"This is my car. I can take you home."

"Why?" She was squinting. "I've lost my sunglasses."

Oh, right. "I could call for a taxi if you would prefer."

"But you know who I am." She wasn't making sense. "I'm sorry," she said. "Any port in a storm."

"What are you saying?"

"Me. Any port in a storm. I don't know how to…"

I waited and waited. "You don't know how to what?"

"Please wait. I don't know how to navigate. To be honest, I don't what I am doing here. If I am cognisant of such a situation, in usual circumstances, I tend to chart a course to relieve me of my burdens. For any port in a storm. Take me for a drive."

No hint of a please there, from a ridiculously verbose woman who went to Roedean and the University of East Anglia no less, but never mind. I opened the door and watched her climb in, my eyes on the shapely legs. I went round to the driver's seat and got in and wondered where I should go. *Any port in a storm.* Just that loaded quote would assure me of the front page of all major newspapers around the world. Why would she tell me that? Didn't her PR people warn her against free speech? And what was she doing in my car? This was surreal. Any marina in a storm. Opposite the Mariners' Club to boot.

I wound past the Sheraton and the mirror-glass buildings of Tsim Sha Tsui East, past small groups of protesters with their yellow umbrellas straggling home after a day blocking major arteries in Kowloon, and through the Cross-Harbour Tunnel which took us to Hong Kong island, supposing that that would be where Marina was staying.

"Take me to the beach."

"To the beach? It's almost three in the morning."

"Take me to the beach."

There's nothing like adult discussion to clear the air, when each side listens and considers.

"All right, then."

I took the Eastern Expressway, skirting Causeway Bay, North Point, Quarry Bay, once home to the waterside offices of the South China Morning Post, and followed the signs to the south of the island. We drove past shops on the ground floor of skyscrapers which in just a few hours would be selling rattan furniture, wedding dresses and red meat laid out on trays under red lamps. Not all in one shop, you understand. In lots of different shops, which all held endless appeal for this Cambridgeshire lad who had made Hong Kong his home fifteen years earlier. We started up the hill of Chaiwan Road, with schools, government offices and a fire station with the bauhinia flag flying on the right, past blocks of flats, pink in the moonlight, on the left. I turned right on to Tai Tam Road, with narrow, lichen-covered concrete steps leading up into thick foliage, the Hong Kong Observatory high above, set appropriately against the stars. The narrow two-way road rose into dense, sweet-smelling vegetation, over hundred-year-old stone bridges spanning brooks and along steep edges falling into lush bracken below. The road started down, views of graves on the distant hillside to the left. Little paths with steep concrete steps ran up and down to isolated villages. Then bigger paths appeared – drives to mansions to the left and right, homes to some of the wealthiest people in the world, one or two of whom proudly announced their names on tidy, white signs. We were in Shek O, a sleepy, dead-end village where rich Chinese and poor Westerners lived cheek by jowl.

I turned right at the roundabout outside a Thai restaurant and parked next to the beach, near a Spartan-looking mini-golf course featuring the Temple of Heaven and other Chinese wonders. It was here, years ago, I made love to a Filipina bar girl, next to the lifeguard hut, and halfway through she threw up. She said something hadn't agreed with her.

Marina and I got out of the car without talking and walked on to the sand. She took off her shoes.

"Who are you?" she asked. She sat down and patted the sand, asking me to sit too. Telling me to sit. This was Marina Makhdoom, sitting next to me, just a few feet from the gently lapping waves. What was going on? "What is your occupation?"

Should I tell her the truth? It could be the end of very short relationship.

"I'm a journalist," I said, looking up at the dark, steep grass hills which rose on the right of the bay.

"First class," she said. "Who with?"

"Shrubs news agency."

"Jubilation. So my little secret is no longer a secret."

"Which little secret is that?"

"Take among many choices. The newspapers have been saying I've left my husband."

"Yes. He's a dentist."

"What? Well none of it is true. I love my husband in perpetuity. I just need some time to think." I turned briefly and caught her wet eyes. "Are you going to write all this down and issue a story?" she asked.

I had a top story on my hands. In the palms of my hands, even. "I just want to help you," I said.

"Yes. You have already. Thank you. I am not even cognisant of your name."

"Hadley."

"I see. Well, Hadley, you know who I am. Why do you wear such heavy, horn-rimmed spectacles?"

"I'm sorry you don't like..."

"Are you trying to look more intelligent than you really are? You look like a mountebank. Have you ever been to Pakistan?"

"Many times."

"I see. Have I had the pleasure of your acquaintance before?"

"No. I would certainly remember if I had met you, but I haven't. I know where you live, though."

She put her hand against her heart. "Is that the threat of the obsessed?"

"I just mean I know where the family home is. On the Margalla Road. Beneath the hills. Near the cricket ground. It is a beautiful part of Islamabad. Islamabad is a beautiful city. Parts of it. I don't really know what I'm saying."

"Don't be nervous. Here, have a drink."

She pulled out a quarter bottle of twelve-year-old Bell's, took a mouthful and offered it to me. I took a swig, realising I was kissing her lips, the inside of her lips even, by proxy. She was looking straight ahead, fidgeting with her fingers.

"Have you met my husband?" she asked.

"No, I haven't. I believe..."

"What do you believe?"

"I hear he is very powerful."

"Yes. Very strong. What was that song they were singing in the bar?"

"Which song?"

"The song they were singing. About a strong man."

"Ah, right. That's an old song. By Rick Astley."

"I like it," she said. "Like my husband."

"Rick Astley is like your husband?"

"The strong man. I like the reference. Do you like it?"

She had hit a bit of a nerve here. It was a favourite of an ex-girlfriend who had left me for a gangster.

"I quite like it," I said. And that slight connection let the words tumble out. "I am not going to write a story about you or tell anyone."

She turned and smiled and I saw the dimples. She put her hand on my knee. "Thank you, Bradley."

"Hadley."

"Thank you, Hadley." Tears bulged in her eyes now. Either she was playing the politician, or my kindness, or desire to prolong the relationship or, who knows, far down the line, the dim prospect of me getting into her pants had made her really sad.

"It isn't in me to let you down," I added. Total, nonsensical capitulation in front of a good-looking woman. "No one would believe me if I told them anyway."

"You can take me back now."

But I didn't want the conversation to be over quite so soon. I shifted in the sand and leant towards her, leaning my head on my elbow. "Marina's a funny old name for a Pakistani," I said.

"Is it," she said. It wasn't a question.

"And any old port in a storm. Any old marina in a storm, more like."

"I see," she said. "You are making a Western play on words at my expense. You have convinced me of your ignorance of Pakistani culture. Take me home."

"Please, don't take offence. I was just trying to break the ice."

"Take me to the Mid-Levels. I will show you where. Then I will say goodbye. No, please be waiting."

"What?"

"Thank you for everything, Mister Hadley. I've changed my mind. You can go now."

"I can go?"

"Yes, I know my way around these parts. Leave me, please."

"But we are at the end of the road here. We are a long way from town. Let me drive you home."

"You can walk with me to the village."

"What's in the village?"

"Come along."

Come along? She wasn't my bloody mother. I followed her

nevertheless, watching her bottom flick from side to side in the expensive jeans which narrowed down to high heels. I breathed in a scent of flowers. We passed the mini-golf course and the roundabout and turned into the village down a narrow road next to the Thai restaurant. She was walking about ten feet in front of me, past the spooky house with tiny windows covered in decades of grime on the left and rounded the corner of an abandoned village house that had been boarded up for years. I stopped in my tracks, slightly pissed off at her just marching ahead and taking me for granted. It must have been all of five seconds, ten at the most, before I too turned the corner to see – nothing.

She had disappeared. She had turned a corner and vanished.

I looked around me. There was a pink and yellow house battened down for the night. She hadn't gone in there. I would have heard her if she had. The house on the corner was a traditional, two-storey "siu chuen nguk" village house which had been abandoned and chained up for as long as I could remember. White board on the front door, brown board on the tiny windows with pretty, rotting, blue wooden frames. Rust dripped off the locks on to utility bills and posters of varying age and repair plastered across the walls. Don't do this, don't do that. "Ground under repair." "Danger." "Planning permission under consideration." "Ice for sale (opposite Thai restaurant)."

"Marina?" I called softly, but not softly enough to stop a dog from barking in reply. The lanes of Shek O are like a model village. Not like a model village in which everything is tidy, mown, manicured and bland and the residents look at you through gaps in the curtains. But a scaled-down model of a village. I was standing within feet of people fast asleep. Where had she gone? I'd heard no car, no voices, no gate opening. No sounds of a struggle. No footsteps. I looked back the way we had come. Someone had told me that the ancient spooky house with the grimy windows was in fact a columbarium, in which the resting place for an urn of ashes cost more in rent per square foot than the most expensive real estate in the world. The cost of dying index.

It occurred to me once again that I had an enormous story on my hands. A career-changing scoop. Not only had I found the missing bloody prima donna princess, I had gone and lost her again. I walked up the hill beyond where Marina had disappeared and stopped. I looked for big holes she might have fallen into, but there weren't any. I looked for ditches under the ancient, tiny, gnarled trees, but again, nothing.

"This is just silly," I said.

I wandered back to the beach, strangely not fearing the worst. I took a swig from my hip flask and sat down on the sand where we had been just minutes before. Why had I told her I wouldn't write a story? What was the matter with me? This was pure gold. I had to be a strong, strong man.

I rang the office where I knew Fagin, the backbone of the desk, was on the overnight shift.

"Fagin? It's Hadley."

"What the fuck do you want?"

"Sorry to interrupt your animal porn channel. I happen to be calling in with a terrific story."

"A story? It's almost four in the morning."

"We could talk about the time. But I would rather give you some copy. Are you ready?"

"Is this some sort of wind-up? Have you been drinking?"

"Are you ready?"

"I am. But if this is some sort of a wind-up..."

"*Pakistani politician Marina Makhdoom...*"

"Wait, you're writing a story about Marina Makhdoom?"

"*Pakistani politician Marina Makhdoom...*"

"Hold on. How do you spell her? M. A. C..."

"M.A.K.H. doom, as in your career prospects. *Pakistani politician Marina Makhdoom, whose whereabouts have been subject to mass media speculation in recent weeks, has turned up in Hong Kong and spent Friday night wining and dining at one of Hong Kong's hottest nightclubs*

"Whoa, laddie. You saw her?"

"I did."

"Totally cool. Where were you?"

"Rick's."

"Rick's?"

"Yes."

"But Hadley, Rick's is a dive."

"Okay. Just say at a Hong Kong nightclub."

"And you saw her wining and dining? Who was she with? That sounds posh."

Fuck me, the Scottish git was right. "Okay... *Pakistani politician Marina Makhdoom, whose whereabouts have been subject to etc etc, has turned up in Hong Kong and spent part of Friday night at a nightclub.*"

"Is 'whereabouts' singular or plural?"

"You mean are 'whereabouts' singular or plural."

"Yes."

"I don't fucking care."

"Go on."

"Second paragraph, nice and brusque: *And then she disappeared again.*"

"What?"

"What's the matter?"

"Marina Makhdoom turns up and then vanishes?"

"Well that's what happened. I was with her, here in Shek O, and then she took off and I don't know where she went."

"Hadley."

"What is it?" I took a mouthful from my hip flask.

"Have you been drinking all night?"

"Fagin, I wouldn't lie to you. This is all true. I have these great quotes. But I am quite tired."

"Well, can't we just say she's turned up in Hong Kong? And

forget about the going missing again. Perhaps she just took a corner somewhere and you didn't see."

"That's exactly what happened. Terrific. You're right. I also have these great quotes."

"Go on."

"Well, I wasn't taking notes, but she said that she hadn't left her husband, as people have been saying, but that she loves him 'in perpetuity'."

"What the fuck does that mean?"

"It's a legal term. Land law, I think. It means she's *never, ever going to give him up* in the words of Rick Astley. She also said 'any port in a storm' and that she finds it difficult to navigate."

"Hadley."

"Yes."

"I don't know what you're on about."

"Well, great. Here I am, giving you a fucking scoop about one of the most famous women on the planet, and all you can say is you don't know what the fuck I am on about."

"Exactly. You were singing just now."

"Well... so where do we go from here?"

"If it's a scoop, why don't you write it up in the morning. Later in the morning, I mean. After due consideration. For instance, I don't suppose she would have said anything had she known you were a journalist."

"I told her I was a journalist!"

"So she said all that was on the record? Any port in a storm, all that?"

"Well not exactly."

"I rest my case."

The bastard was right. I would sleep. Then I would try to find her. Then I would write my story. I lay back, closed my eyes and thought about drinking from her bottle.

I WOKE TO THE SOUND of happy people. The beach was filling up fast.

So early in the day? I looked at my watch. It was already ten. I was crumpled and drained and my neck hurt and I badly needed a wash. I bought a toothbrush and toothpaste at a convenience store and rinsed myself in the cold shower next to the car park, using a cleanish rag from the car as a towel. I went back into the village and stood at the spot where Marina had vanished. The ancient brick wall of the abandoned house and a chained gate on one side, and impenetrable foliage and a wall on the other.

A middle-aged gweilo walked past with an unkempt dog.

"I'm sorry," I said. "Have you seen a young Pakistani woman around here?"

He looked around sheepishly and said: "I am afraid my dog has been in the long grass and will be covered in ticks. Come along, Baxter."

So the nutter brigade was out early, then. And this particular nutter had a dog with the same name, and not a common one at that, as my news editor.

I sat at the Thai restaurant with no walls, overlooking the roundabout, breathing in the scent of sea. There's nothing pretty about Shek O in the sense of a prim English village. There are tarpaulins, wires, scrappy corrugated tin roofs, tall, tatty hoardings advertising Coke and seafood, and traffic signs and antennae sprouting up everywhere. But the overall impression is that of harmony. I felt a Paul McCartney song coming on and had to put a stop to that straight away. A Chinese workman in his sixties, dressed in white with white flour or plaster on his face and wearing a green cowboy hat, walked past, followed by a black stray dog with white feet, its head held high. Then came another old man on a child's bicycle with an old-fashioned car horn on the handlebar. He went round the roundabout and back the way he had come, giving me a smile as he passed. Up in the scarred green hills the other side of the beach, a tiny man was jumping up and down and waving his arms. None of my business. I turned to look inside the restaurant to signal for a beer. The owners were sitting round a table chopping vegetables as their children did their homework. A grandmother was bouncing a baby on her lap. I felt totally relaxed. In fact, so relaxed, that I stopped worrying about Marina. My phone rang. An unknown number.

"Hello?"

I could hear traffic in the background, but there was no voice. The phone rang off. Then it rang again. I answered but did not say anything. I could hear the traffic noise. Then a man started to sing from a distance. He wasn't singing "From a Distance", but was singing from a long way away. It was a loud, echoing sound, starting low and rising. It was the Muslim call to prayer from a crackling loudspeaker.

"Hello?" I said.

The phone cracked as if changing hands, and as if it were a really crap phone.

"Hello?" a man said.

"Hello."

A long pause, and then: "Be my servant." That's what it sounded like anyway, in a strange unplaceable accent.

"Sorry?"

"Be my servan-ter." And that was exactly how it sounded. Be my servant with an extra syllable and extra emphasis. And it was sung in a kind of a chant, like the Magnificat or Te Deum, except there was the Muslim call to prayer in the background.

"I'm sorry this is a really bad line..."

It was so bad that the man at the other end hung up.

CHAPTER TWO

Shrubs news agency has its Asian headquarters on the twenty-third floor of an office overlooking the harbour with the Kowloon hills in the distance and mainland China beyond. I sat at my desk, closed my eyes and tried to relax. I had had a bizarre and personal exchange with one of the most famous women in Asia and every time I thought about it my heart skipped a beat. It was like revisiting a dream. I had told Fagin to keep schtum about it until I had decided what to do. After all, I had told her I wouldn't write a thing. Why did I do that? She was a spoilt army brat who could twist men round her little finger. I should have been banging out my story right now, telling anyone who approached: "You're not going to *believe* this." But I had promised her I would censor myself. Why? There was zero chance I would ever get to see her again. She would have woken up around two in the afternoon and thought: "Fuck me, that was a lucky escape. Meeting the only journalist on the planet who didn't know a perfect story when it kicked him in the balls." Then she would have taken a couple of Alka-Seltzers and gone back to sleep.

I did know the perfect story, as long as I could get someone to corroborate it. It couldn't just be me going on about me meeting her. It was a tough one. But I would be a star, even though, recently, I had been thinking of getting off this "general news" beat and writing about the tea market and becoming an expert. Something less fraught, anyway, though I hadn't quite thought it through. Shrubs wasn't going to pay me to write solely about tea. But I wanted to do something simpler and more relaxing, to wander slowly around cool plantations in the highlands of India, Sri Lanka and Malaysia asking Tamil girls how they knew when the leaf was ripe to pluck. And then I would sit down to a nice cuppa on the veranda of some plantation with the owner and his smoking-hot wife and talk about aroma. As I said, I hadn't thought it through.

"Hadley? You look awful."

My dream was broken by my bright and perky news editor, Rodney Baxter, the aroma of whose perky aftershave troubled my stomach as I returned to work on the Monday, starting at the unearthly hour of midday.

"Thanks, Rodney. Couple of late nights."

"Why am I not surprised?"

"Can't answer that, Rodney."

"Well, sorry to have to make you work, now you're here in the office. Can you give me a few graphs on this?"

He dropped a print-out on my desk. It was an emailed press release from the Pakistan Consulate. It was a statement about Marina. I read the top – Marina had not gone missing, it said. She was visiting a sick relative in Hong Kong. Ah. I had been scooped.

"I could give it to the Hong Kong bureau, but they don't know the story as well as you," Baxter said. "And Islamabad haven't opened yet."

"Sure. Leave it with me."

"Also throw in some of the stuff from the papers. Lots of sightings of her in the bars but no solid sources."

"Sure. Rodney?"

"What is it?"

"Nothing."

"Where were you last night, by the way?"

"Usual places. Friday night was the long one."

"What's the matter with you, Hadley? I'm sure if you had been on the ball you could have found her at one of your usual places. Maybe you could have bought her a drink. Had a little dance." Rodney cackled. "But then again, maybe her usual places are different from your usual places."

"Definitely."

Towards the bottom of the consulate statement it said Marina was expected to contest the next general election and to run for office as the new leader of the Pakistan Popular Party.

"Leave it with me," I said.

Hong Kong had its own bureau, but they were so busy with the democracy protests and financial markets that a lot of their news was handled on the editing desk. This was a pretty boring story, to tell the truth. So she was expected to do all this. That wasn't news. What was news was that I seemed to know a lot more about what Marina was up to in Hong Kong than the consulate did. But where had she gone? I had a sudden bout of the collywobbles, thinking that maybe, after all, she had been abducted, but I didn't really believe that. Shek O is home to a pretty eclectic bunch of people, rich and poor, Chinese and white, Pakistani and Thai. She could have slipped into anyone's home. Maybe a boyfriend's. That would be it. That's why she asked to go to the beach.

"Marina Makhdoom."

This was Marcus, who was sitting opposite me with a wet, supercilious smile on his ginger face. He had his feet on the desk and his keyboard on his lap, chewing gum and leering all at the same time. He was handsome in a T.E. Lawrence sort of way and always smelt of incense and dope. He was a dope.

"What about her?" said Fagin, with a glance in my direction.

Marcus looked up. "You would, right?" He leered around the desk. "I mean, Marina Makhdoom." No one said anything. "I mean, you wouldn't say no."

"Wouldn't say no to what, Marcus?" Fagin asked.

"Yeah, right."

"You have to learn to shut the fuck up when no one wants you to speak," Fagin said. "You have to learn not to be a ginger fuck."

"Fuck off, Fagin," Marcus said, turning to me. "Hadley, you won't believe this, but there was this girl last week."

A tawdry, ginger dope fuck and he was right. I wasn't going to believe him.

"Leave me alone, Marcus.'

"There was this girl," he said again. "In KL. You won't believe what she said."

"What did she say? Did she say hello? Was she a waitress? Did she ask you what you wanted to drink?"

"Don't be a prat. You'll never guess."

I didn't say anything. I didn't want to encourage him. *Be my servant,* the man had said on the phone. What was that all about?

"Hadley?"

"Yes."

"You'll never guess what she said to me."

"You're right. I'll never guess. No point trying."

"Go on. Take a guess. I was in KL. For the election. Only got back this morning. She followed me out of the office to the lift. She looked me in the eye and said it."

"All right, what did she say?"

"Take a guess."

"Which floor please?"

"What? No. Be serious. She said it in a whisper, making sure we were alone."

"What did she say?"

"Sotto voce like, if you know what I mean."

"What did she say, Marcus?"

"She said... she said: 'Any time, any place.'"

Marcus looked at me, waiting for me to react.

"Any time, any place?"

"That's what she said."

"What did she mean?"

"What?"

"She was talking about the wi-fi? The reception?"

"No, you prick. She meant..."

"What?"

"Hadley, what do you think she meant?"

"She was talking about her smart phone," Fagin said.

"No. She meant I could... you know. Any time, any place."

"Well did you?"

"Well no, actually."

"So how do you that was what she meant? That's not a very good story."

"Oh fuck off. You just want to put everyone down, don't you, Hadley? You want to crush every initiative."

"This was an initiative? Yours or hers?"

"Get fucked."

"Any time any place."

But I was interested to find out who she was. I mean, if she had said that to Marcus, the world's most dysfunctional person, maybe ... I called up the Shrubs online staff directory.

"Marcus, sorry man," I said. "I was just taking the piss." I called up the Malaysia directory. I called up the "colleagues" page and clicked "large icons". I was skimming through pictures of all the women in the KL office. There was a complete beauty called Isabella in TV.

"Who said it?" I asked.

"What?"

"Who said 'any time, any place' to you in the Kuala Lumpur office?"

There was a cutie in the pictures department called Mei-mei who was looking at the camera through lowered eye-lashes. An intern on the reporting side looked foxy, but way too young. For me or Marcus.

"Why do you ask?" Marcus asked.

I smiled. "I mean, it's such a good line. I just wanted..."

"You want to meet her."

"Don't be silly, I just wanted to know…" Come to think of it, the bureau chief was hot too. Her name, according to the caption, was Bernard Botsford.

Baxter came out of his office looking smug. He came up behind Marcus and put his hands on the sunken shoulders as Marcus sat up straight and replaced his keyboard on the desk.

"This man," Baxter said loudly, now patting both Marcus's shoulders and beaming at the other deskers. "This man is hopeless, lonely and sad. A complete waste of space. Keep up the good work. All of you."

Just a little snippet of conversation on the desk. Probably not a fair representation, but not far off. Baxter wasn't finished.

"As for you, Hadley, I want you to pop down to Shek O with pix and TV. We have a story on our hands."

"Marina?"

"What?" asked Baxter.

"You would, wouldn't you?" said Marcus.

"Fuck off, Marcus," I said. "What's the story, Rodney? Anything about Marina Makhdoom?"

"What makes you think it's anything about Marina Makhdoom? You're writing a story about her. You've got her on the brain."

"Sorry," I said. "What's the story?"

"The protests. There's a new Occupy Central protest zone, except it's not in Central."

"It's on the beach?"

"Exactly, my old China. Take TV and pix. Some prick also called up to say there are crops circles sprouting up all over the shop."

"Crop circles?"

"In all the rolling wheat fields, apparently."

"Is this prick a reliable prick?"

"Haven't a clue. But I want you to check it out all the same.

The Hong Kong file is looking a little thin. You could do with some fresh air. And if you run into Marina Makhdoom, please don't be shy about asking her what she is doing and why she is giving everyone the run-around."

So there I was on my way back down to rural Shek O – twice in three days – when the last time I had visited before that was about two years earlier. But Shek O wasn't rural in the sense of crops. There were no rolling fields of wheat or sorghum, that was the point. Baxter was being heavily sarcastic. There were the hills and a glorious greener-than-green golf course for the super rich with little hump-backed bridges across streams. The only things that rolled were the expats off the hundred-miles-per-hour double-decker buses at the art deco terminus after a night making a fool of themselves in the bars of Wanchai.

"We're off to the coast to see some crop circles," I said to the young visuals team waiting for me in the lobby. "Isn't it a nice day?"

We took the same route Marina and I had taken that Saturday morning, over the hill and down into the dead-end village, the shops now alive with wedding dresses and red meat under red lampshades. There were one or two protesters walking the opposite direction to us, dressed in yellow, one or two carrying the trademark yellow umbrellas, but when we reached the village, there was nothing. One or two protesters at the Thai restaurant, that was all.

"So was there a big turnout?" I asked one girl.

"No big turnout," she said. "We think we were mistaken."

So I called the desk and said the protest lead was all bollocks and went instead to the house of the family which had raised the alarm (the only family to have raised the alarm) about crop circles. This was a lovely part of the job. The main story is out of the way, either written or a bust like today, and you had a couple of hours to spend drinking or wasting your time with a silly 200-word story about crop circles.

The family lived in a tall, narrow, white house, built like a tug, behind the bus station in the main street where someone had written "how old were you when you found out that Santa Claus was real?" in chalk. The man was Macau-Portuguese, at a guess, and was wearing shorts and t-shirt and smoking a roll-up. He had a big smile and glassy eyes, raising alarm bells with me and my young pictures and TV colleagues. I heard the TV woman mumble something rude in Cantonese under her breath. I turned and winked at her. Why I winked, I had no idea.

"We saw a circle in the hills, and then on the golf course and then on the beach," the man said, drawing hard on his cigarette.

"On the beach?"

"Like a line, a series of lines in the sand? Totally heavy."

"You saw lines in the sand and thought they were crop circles?"

The man looked to his wife for support. "They were animal crops. In the sand," she said. "Circles in the crops."

"What?"

"Don't listen to her," the man said. "She's barmy. But it was the golf course that convinced me."

"What did you see?"

"Circles that could not have been made by nature."

"Go on."

"They were green, but totally awesome. A different green to the grass all around."

"Perfect circles!" the woman shouted from the kitchen. "Explain that!"

"Hadley," the TV camerawoman said.

"What is it?"

"Can I have a word?"

"What is it?"

"What do you fucking think?" She turned to the man and asked slowly: "Is the grass very short in these crop circles?"

"Praise the lord. You've seen them too?"

"I think so. And have you seen little flags in the middle of them?"

"Markers of some sort, we thought. Though markers in what dimension, we have no clue," the man said. "There. Your friend bears witness."

"Hadley, let's go."

"So you called us all the way down here to say you've seen greens on the golf course?" I asked.

"It is not a game with which I am familiar," he said. "But the circles are still there. If you turn right at the…"

"And they just sprang up overnight?" I asked.

"We never said they had just sprung up," the man said. "They have been there a long time. And each time my wife and I passed them, we felt we were in the presence of something larger than ourselves."

"Yup, you got that bit right."

"We were afraid of what they portended."

"I see," I said. "Well, I can tell you. They portended a wasted trip down to Shek O and they portended us leaving right now."

"I have some other news."

"Really," I said.

"Oh yes. But perhaps that won't interest you either."

"Well try us."

The man looked towards his wife again. She came through wiping the back of her neck with a towel.

"Marina Makhdoom. The Pakistani woman. So many stories about where she might be and how she may have left her husband."

"Yes?"

"Well, we've seen her in the village."

"You have?"

"A couple of times."

"What was she doing?"

"Well, she was with a famous Pakistani sportsman, we are told. A player of cricket."

"Cricket?"

"It is not a game with which I am familiar."

"Like golf, you mean. What was she doing? Was it Ian Botham?"

"Calm down, Hadley." This was the TV woman again. She was in her mid-twenties but behaving much in a much more grown up fashion than me. I realized that straight away.

"Who?" the man asked.

"Would you recognize his name if I said it?" I asked.

"He was Pakistani too," the woman said. "They looked like they were very close."

"Freddie Flintoff," I said.

"Hadley, he was Pakistani," the TV woman said.

"He was older than her," the man said.

"Saleem Malik. Javed Miandad."

"Very good looking," the woman said. "Smoldering."

"Imran Khan!"

"Hadley, calm down."

"Older than Imran Khan," the woman said. "I know who Imran Khan is."

"Older? It's not possible!" I said.

"I mean a very, very famous cricketer. More famous than Imran Khan. Mian someone."

"Mian Langhari?"

"That's him."

"But the man must be seventy," I said.

"Well, they were very lovey-dovey," she said.

"He's old enough to be her father!"

"Hadley, calm..."

"Where did they go?" I was talking to the man.

"Well that's the funny thing..."

"What's so funny?"

The TV camerawoman punched my arm hard.

"I'm sorry," I said. "But please tell us where you saw

Makhdoom and Langhari."

"We followed them from the beach," the woman said. "We were going to say hello. We were going to tell them about the crop circles."

"We were walking up from the Thai restaurant on the corner, on the road to the point," the man said. "We turned a corner and they had simply disappeared."

"What do you mean they simply disappeared?"

"I mean just that. We turned a corner, by the run-down house with boarded-up windows and the posters and signs for ice from the Thai restaurant. They had vanished."

Pulling a second disappearing act, with a very old man to boot. I had read somewhere that Langhari had to get up twice in the night to wee.

I LIVE IN TAI PO in the New Territories, next to a flower farm, away from the hustle and bustle of Hong Kong island and the braying expats who work for banks and spend all day complaining about their maids. I had moved just a couple of weeks earlier from the outlying island of Lamma, with its glorious beaches, ugly power station, dodgy hippies, frowning journalists and the grave of an English croupier. Propped up in my ancient Mercedes, I followed an open-topped truck carrying all my belongings to my new home. There in front, flickering in the sunlight through the arching trees overhead, were my custom-made rattan filing cabinet, my rattan sofa with the curved corners and arm chairs with the white cushions and a fold-down rosewood desk. I was following my sitting room at speed down a narrow country lane which ran along the side of the Kowloon-Canton Railway. Extraordinary.

The house was similar to my place on Lamma, but this one had two usable roofs surrounded by waist-high walls with lights in each corner. It was perfect for barbecues, but who was going to travel all the way out to see me? No one. Let's be honest. I was a long, long way away from the Hong Kong most people knew (even the people who lived here) in a tiny village surrounded by misty brown hills and graves on one side and kumquat and peach blossom trees on the other.

I stood on the lower roof, about ten-foot square, and looked across hundreds of pots of kumquat trees, four foot tall and perched on bamboo shelves. Chinese buy them for good luck in the run-up to the lunar new year (the orange kumquats, which shine like bright blobs of paint when seen from the road, look like gold and symbolise wealth). They would all be gone within a few weeks – all except those, now lying on their sides, that were so small, spindly and frail that they didn't symbolise wealth so much as serious ill health. Death, even.

In the middle of the flower farm, about a hundred yards away, was an old, one-storey house with a tin roof, its whitewashed walls green with lichen and damp. A girl dressed in black, wearing a broad-rimmed Hakka hat, was playing with a puppy tied to a window latch on a long piece of string. I cracked open a beer and lit a cigarette and watched. Ancient China alive, oblivious and happy in bustling twenty-first century Hong Kong.

Someone knocked at the door two floors down, for fuck's sake. Just as I was alone, relaxed and about to get happily drunk. I looked over the roof wall and down at the alley.

Marina Makhdoom was sitting on the concrete doorstep with her back to the building. I didn't say anything. I stood back from the wall, mouthed *fuck* to myself and pumped my right fist gently in the air. What was she doing here, a million miles from anywhere diplomatic and city-like?

I skipped downstairs to the bathroom and gargled with mouthwash. I skipped to the next room, the kitchen, and took a swig of Black Label to disguise the smell of peppermint. I skipped downstairs again, to the ground floor, happy as could be, answered the door and tried really hard to look surprised.

"My goodness. Mrs Makhdoom?"

She was standing up, a cigarette now in her hand, and she turned and… didn't give me a smile.

"Let me pass," she said.

"Of course."

She climbed the first flight of stairs, walked left through the hundred-square-foot living room, with the rattan furniture and Bose speakers right now playing John Prine's "Oldest Baby in the World", and turned left again up the second flight to the roof.

"Please do come right on in," I said as I struggled to keep pace. Every time I say something like that, I realise it is *dripping* in English sarcasm, and I hate myself for using it on the other side of the world. But there you are.

I turned through the thickly painted red door and saw her standing, her hands pressed down on the hip-high wall like a snooker player, looking down at where she had been sitting seconds earlier.

"Don't do it," I said. It was a joke.

She turned, a wild look in her eye, her hair a trifle… wild, and pointed her cigarette at me.

"If you're wondering how I found you, Pakistan has an intelligence service second to none."

Her first line of normal conversation and it was a plug for Pakistan's Inter-Services Intelligence agency, though second to none didn't sound like a very good score. One below zero. Things weren't looking up.

"That must be very reassuring," I said. "If you ever get lost." She didn't say anything, but leant her head on one side like a Labrador. "But why do they keep tabs on me?" I asked.

"Because you are a journalist and you have been to Pakistan many times. And they would have seen you take me away from that bar."

"It was hardly an abduction. They were watching you?"

"Yes, of course. Then they were watching both of us. I called them. A contact. I just asked: where does the motherfucker live?

And here I am."

"I see. Are they watching us now? I mean, are they watching you and the, um, motherfucker?"

"Behind me, across the fruit farm and the flowers, there is an elevated highway, no?"

"Yes."

"It's on a curve and there is no stopping allowed."

"That is true."

"And yet there are two white SUVs pulled up and two men looking over the concrete wall at us with binoculars."

"Goodness," I said again, using a word I rarely use twice in the matter of a minute. "How did you do that? How do you know?"

"I can see the reflection in your eyes."

"Oh wow. Would they care to come in for some tea?"

"What?"

"Or something stronger, perhaps. They are on a dangerous bend after all. Trucks carrying pigs from China come round that corner at a fair old clip."

It struck me that I was talking complete nonsense. Like a love-struck Hugh Grant behind the blue door and in front of the fridge in "Notting Hill".

"They know how to handle themselves," Marina said.

"Oh, right."

"I just called to say," she said, stubbing out her cigarette on the until-now really clean wall tiles. "I just called here to say thank you."

"For what?"

"For rescuing me the other night."

"It was my pleasure. Really. It was an honour to meet you."

"And it may be possible to see you in Pakistan, Hadley. May it be possible?"

"Well..."

"Shrubs sends in helpers and assistants for elections, surely? Why don't you volunteer to be a helper?"

A couple of things struck me as remarkable here: a few moments ago she had referred to me as a motherfucker and now she was saying she wanted to see me again. She had also remembered my name and the name of my company, unless she was being fed lines into some device in her ear by the two men on the road.

"Please give the concept due consideration," she said.

"I will. Is there going to be an election?"

"There will be an election and I expect I will be running as behoves the leader of the party. I am a Makhdoom. Ipso facto, I am most encouraged and likely to become the next part leader. Those efficient and able security men are picking me up at the end of your village. Please don't see me out."

She put out her hand for me to shake, which I did. She stood looking me in the eyes for a good four seconds (I tried to count them later). She pulled her hand away slowly, her fingers reaching round my hand to my knuckles and giving them what seemed to be a bit of a stroke. And then, with a slow clatter of metal and heels and bangles swishing against porcelain tiles, she was out through the metal door and down two flights of stairs and into the sun-caked alleyway.

"Bye," I said cheerily from the roof. She didn't look back. She went up four mossy steps and down four mossy steps, leant against a hundred-year-old stone hut full of kindling wood, lifted a shoe and inspected the heel and was off again, head down, until she reached the road and looked around for her car. Then she waved at someone, presumably the ISI guys, out of my line of vision, and then, only then, did she turn and give me a brief wave.

"Bye," I said to myself. She disappeared from sight. How strange, I thought. I hadn't asked where she had vanished to that night, this woman so lacking in confidence and self-esteem. Ipso facto, indeed. And I hadn't asked her about the ancient cricketer.

I went downstairs, poured a large Scotch, lit a cigarette, turned up the music, walked through to the tiny bathroom, looked in the mirror – and beamed. Thinking back to that moment gives me the collywobbles. She could have looked back straight away and then got on with the business at hand of finding her car. That would have proved an attention span of a few seconds. But no. She had walked all the way to the road and *then* looked back. She had been thinking about me all the time I was looking after her as she climbed the four steps and climbed down four more. That is the mad logic of a man obsessed, if not in love. I can now, at a moment's notice, summon the sights and sounds of that day, apart from the feeling of her stroking the back of my hand. Shadows on the alleyway from the sun behind the globe lights on my roof. The deafening cicadas from the flower farm. The girl in her black Hakka pyjamas playing with her dog. I can smell the chicken frying in the rusting iron wok next door with the woman's clatter and a curse. I once had a wok like that. It broke into pieces like a biscuit.

CHAPTER THREE

THE GUNMEN APPEARED at the top of the hill in a line. Glints of sunlight on either their knives, stirrups or bridles gave them away in the few seconds before they started down in a cloud of dust, heading for the train. On flatter ground, their horses stepped up their canter into a gallop and they were gaining on the ancient steam engine called the Empress of India, which someone earlier had said was only "good for shunting". The riders were approaching fast. I could hear their shouting over the noise of the train. The only hope was to reach the railway tunnel before the horses reached the train.

"Oh, that's a bit of luck!" someone shouted. "This is the Bindar Tunnel. It's over two miles long!"

I hit the pause button and stopped the passing flight attendant for another large gin and tonic. I was a bit brusque, I admit, but it was only a couple of hours before we landed in Islamabad. And she had ignored me twice before and I was keen to get back to "North West Frontier" and see if Kenneth More, Lauren Bacall et al could hold the bandits off. All I could remember about the 1960 film was the sinister Herbert Lom, a Dutch-Indonesian Muslim, who had tried to stick the Hindu prince's hand into a fast-spinning water pump wheel which had made the slow-witted Kenneth More a bit suspicious.

"You British never do anything until you have had tea," Bacall said in one of the film's less gripping moments when it reverts to stereotype. And, truth be known, I wasn't up to doing much until that gin and tonic had arrived. The irony was that this was British India, and North West Frontier was now in Pakistan where I was headed. Except North West Frontier Province had since been renamed Khyber Pakhtunkhwa, which didn't run off the tongue in quite the same way or evoke quite the same sense of history for a poncy Brit who had watched the movie when he was about six with his dad on a Sunday afternoon and thought it was the most exciting film he had ever seen.

One of the key "takeaways" seeing it now was that the conflict was simple. Black and white. At least that was the way the movie made it out to be.

"The rebels are Muslim," a British consular official, Sir Poncy-Ponsonby, told his guests. "They are after the little prince who is a Hindu."

A-hah. Now I understood! But you would have thought all gathered in the room at the time, key players in the affairs of the region one way or another, including Kenneth More and Lauren Bacall, would have known that. Basic background information. Or was there a sub-plot? Were they all suffering from dementia?

Getting the Pakistan election gig turned out to be easier that I had expected. I thought I would have to let Baxter in on a bit of the stuff about Marina, how I had found her and how she had suggested I go to Pakistan to help out. But in the end there was no need.

"I've been thinking about my future," I had told him in his office overlooking the harbour. "I would like to turn my attention to the tea industry."

"Tea?" he asked. "You want to write about tea?"

"I have a feeling it would be very pleasant. Interesting and less stressful."

"Have you entirely lost your mind? Tea? No one just writes about tea. You would have to write the tea market reports, which is a job for an intern. Look, the Pakistan elections are coming up. Why don't you reinforce for a couple of weeks and see how you feel when you get back?"

You fill in forms on the plane before landing in Islamabad which never get collected by the pot-bellied officials, all men, who greet you on arrival. It's a dead giveaway, a time-consuming and vital sign of the health of Pakistan's economy: poor and deteriorating and pushing women aside. Benazir Bhutto Airport is about the same size and has the same technical advantages as the airport in Casablanca. The movie, I mean. I have never been to Casablanca and have no idea what the real airport is like. Perhaps it is totally wired, gleams like crystal and is run by women.

I was picked up by our young office driver, Sultan (emphasis on the second syllable), who didn't like Brits but thought I was okay. He liked the fact that I didn't shout at him as apparently Gary, the Islamabad bureau chief who hadn't been writing many stories recently, and his predecessor had.

"How is Gary?" I asked.

"Mister Gary is always out meeting sources."

"He must be very busy. Can you take me to the Margalla Road?"

"Sure. Can. But now it is very dark."

"That's okay. Can we drive by Marina Makhdoom's house?"

"Sure. No problem. Maybe there will be a light in her room. Like a beacon."

"A beacon?"

"A beacon of hope. For Pakistan."

We took a scrappy highway into town, passed a tell-tale queue of at least a hundred taxis waiting in line to fill up with gas which seemed to get scarcer by the year. The drivers would be there for hours, pushing their cars forward by hand to save fuel as they inched closer. Five men wearing the traditional, white, baggy shalwar kameez were playing cricket under a streetlight on a broad section of road, using bricks as stumps. We headed up the road towards the white Faisal Mosque with its four, pencil-like minarets, negotiating two security checkpoints where sleepy soldiers waved us through. We turned right on the Margalla Road, the forested foothills of the Himalayas on the left and the rich, mostly ugly, cement houses set back from the road on the right, many with the nameplates of doctors on the front gates under towering trees.

Sultan slowed as we passed Marina's family home. All the lights were off. Two guards sat on stools outside the metal gate, their backs bent as they stared out at the hills.

"All sleepy," he said.

"It would appear so."

He took me to a guesthouse called Chateau Hill, Shrubs avoiding the top hotels for security reasons. Reinforcing staff used to stay at the Islamabad Grand with its high teas of hummus and pita bread and grim basement bar, but that all ended when a truck bomb exploded outside the front door, killing dozens and splintering trees on the other side of the road which are somehow still standing.

We turned down the tree-lined Ataturk Avenue, no more than a picturesque lane on the way to the Grand, which had no street lights. And suddenly a mammoth truck, with no headlights, was in our path, swerving at the last second to pass us. I remembered this about Pakistan. Electricity, whether from a grid, a foul-smelling generator or a 12-volt car battery, was used frugally, if at all. Blackouts happened every day, for hours at a time.

The guesthouse was a large building set back from Aga Khan Road with the same tall metal gate and guards. Next to the gate, in between Chateau Hill and the next house, was an electricity junction box about chest high and a foot deep. Actually these boxes are all over the city, varying in size but always in the same state of disrepair. Its door had been forced open and left dangling from a hinge. The wires had been ripped out violently, the meters smashed. It was if it had been attacked by crazed, naked Hollywood zombies.

Inside the hall, a man stood upright behind a tiny counter.

Three men sat upright on hard wooden chairs doing absolutely nothing. The upright standing man was handsome in a quiet, self-effacing South Asian way, with swept back grey hair.

"Hello, there," I said. "I believe you have a reservation for me? Shrubs."

He slapped down my key, a big, clunky affair with a wooden attachment six inches long, on the counter. He must have been holding it all the time. He looked a bit pissed off, truth be told.

"Room twenty-one," I said. "And where might that be?"

The man raised his eyebrows and looked up the stairs briefly.

"Your company instructed us to reserve a room at the rear of the building. What with all these bombs going off everywhere." He waved his fingers in front of his face and made an "I'm so scared" face.

"Right," I said. "Thank you."

The room was large and poor. Two minutes after entering, when I was unwrapping my secretly stowed bottle of scotch they hadn't caught at the airport, a man burst through a door I had assumed was a cupboard. He was carrying an ironing board under his arm. He bowed and left without saying a word.

I went easy on the scotch, knowing that when that was gone, it was just dodgy wine and beer in dodgier bars and restaurants at risk of attack by frenzied Islamist militants. I did that "ooh, scary" thing with my fingers like the man at the desk. I sent emails to the Pakistan bureau chief and the Hong Kong desk saying that I had arrived and watched some CNN. Before going to bed, I opened the door to the first-floor hall which had a pink pool table and a door out to a balcony. No one there. I went to the head of the stairs and looked down. No one there. Complete silence.

I bolted my door, locked the scotch away in my case, washed the glass and went to bed, reminding myself to spray some deodorant around the room in the morning to get rid of a night of whisky breath. The air-conditioner was noisy but consistently so and I was falling asleep when I heard tapping. Was it on the door, on the wall, or in that cupboard which the man had come out of and which I had not investigated? I sat up. It was a light tapping at first, and then a louder banging as if someone was hitting a wooden pole gently against an empty cement mixer. When that stopped, there was the sound of a kettle boiling and then someone banging out a beat with his hands on a table top.

I had been in dangerous situations before. I had been shot at in Afghanistan and waited for a bus at midnight in Stoke Newington. There was always a certain *frisson* when visiting Islamabad, because, beautiful as it was, there was no telling when it was going to turn ugly. I had no idea what was going through the minds of the silent staff of Chateau Hill, for instance.

My phone rang.

"Hadley?"

"Yes?"

"This is Gary."

"Oh, hi."

"Welcome to Islamabad."

"Thanks. It's good to be back."

"You've been here before?"

"Yes. When Benazir was elected."

"Oh right. Fucking decades ago. Well look, there's a party tonight at a Belgian diplomat's place. Plenty of booze."

"Wow. It's two in the morning."

"It'll go on all night. Sultan can drive you."

"I'll tell you what. I'll take a rain cheque. Next time. It's already five in the morning Hong Kong time."

"Wuss."

The line went dead.

"Welcome to Islamabad," I said into the darkness.

I turned on the light and the noises came again. In the same order. I was going to have to look in the cupboard. That sounds silly, but there had been a man in there not such a long time ago.

Who knew who was still in there? Maybe that was his home. Maybe the man had returned via a back entrance. Maybe the cupboard was not so much a cupboard as a vast holding area for Islamist terrorists waiting for the infidel English journalist to fall asleep. And then they would come out, one by one, with giant, gleaming meat hooks in their hands and…

I approached the cupboard. Don't be such a baby.

I opened the door and lit my cigarette lighter. It was bigger than a normal cupboard, for sure. The size of a garden shed. But there was no one inside. There were coils of hosing, half used cans of paint, a sewing machine and two sacks of rice. Not so scary then. I closed the door and went back to bed.

The noise started again. The light tapping, the banging of a tumbler dryer, silence for a while, then the hissing kettle and someone drumming a beat on a table. I would sleep for five minutes and wake up. Why don't you go and try to find out its source? Because it was four in the morning and I was scared, that's why.

But of course, in the light of day, thinks look much brighter. I had breakfast alone, with the young waiter, his head bowed, managing to take my order without saying a word.

"Excuse me," I asked as he was walking away. He turned. "I couldn't help notice there was an awful lot of noise last night. Coming from the next room, perhaps?"

The waiter pointed upstairs.

"Yes, that's right," I said.

He bowed and turned away. The grey-haired manager arrived a minute later. He seemed in a much better mood this morning. Maybe he had had some fantastic sex in the night. That could explain some of the noises. But sex with whom?

"Good morning, Mister Arnold. Has there been some disturbance in the night?"

"Well, yes, I am afraid there has." I was so tired.

"Let me take this opportunity of saying how sorry I am. What example of disturbance?"

"Well, I am not too sure. A lot of banging."

"Banging, you say?"

"Yes. Did you hear it?"

"I can't say that I did. It sounds most serious. But I seldom spend the night on the premises."

"Did you spend last night on the premises?"

"Oh yes. First class. I wouldn't have missed it for the world."

"Missed what for the world?"

"Last night."

Lordy, lordy. "But did you hear anything?"

"Was it the banging of hands? Like this?" He beat out a slow rhythm on the table.

"No, it was more like this." I beat out a faster rhythm, more like a drum roll.

"It is possible the water geyser was playing up. But I heard nothing."

"Well, it went on all night."

"Let me just say this, sir. If it happens again..." He pulled out a pen from his jacket and was writing on the napkin. "... call me on this number. No matter what time, I will come to your room for assistance."

"You'll come to my room?"

"No matter what time. And we can investigate together."

"Well, I hope there won't be a need for that."

"But I am here if the need is great. Any time, any place."

"Oh don't you start."

"Start what?"

"Nothing, sorry. I was thinking out loud. It's just an expression."

My phone rang. It was our Thai photographer, Palakorn, known in the business as "the snappers' snapper", that's how good he was. I had never worked with him. Marina was electioneering in Peshawar and he wanted to go ASAP. The snappers' snapper was picking me up in five minutes.

AND WHOOSH, WE WERE immediately and snappily in action, heading west for the ancient city of Peshawar, beyond which was lawless tribal land heading into the Khyber Pass. Years earlier, a Westerner could pass through to Torkham, the Afghan border crossing. Now it was much too dangerous.

"A Westerner, Mister Hadley, like you – he would be shot dead and hung up like a dog," Sultan said, looking at me in his mirror. He ran his forefinger across his throat and made a "kerr-rick" noise and laughed.

Very funny man. Why would I be hung up like a dog? What was the Islamic hatred of dogs all about? Who would want to hang one anywhere?

"Where's Gary?" I asked,

"Out meeting sources."

We drove though barren, dusty fields dotted with brick factories apparently made of mud with satanic, circular kilns and tapering chimneys belching out smoke. Girls in bright headgear carried piles of the finished product in rows in sub-Dickensian squalor. We came off the highway, passed the five-star Pearl-Continental Hotel, bombed in 2009 and since rebuilt, and turned left into a long straight street of busy traffic where immediately our fancy four-wheel drive was a stationary sore thumb, taller, brighter and prouder than all the other cars, taxis, buses and horse-pulled carriages around us.

"We are a shooting target," Sultan said.

"What do you mean?"

"We should have driven old shit car. This is the road where they see us. They radio ahead. They say we are a shooting target."

"You mean a sitting duck."

"Yes. A sitting shooting target duck. They arrange men on rooftops, on motorcycles. They warn their friends by phone. This is not good."

"So what do we do?"

"There is nothing to do. We cannot move."

Well, maybe not, but if I made a dash for it, I could skedaddle back to the Pearl-Continental and order a stiff G&T by the pool. Just joking. That wouldn't be allowed. I looked out the window. There was a sign for sanitary pipeware above a shop selling DVDs with posters of movies starring men in their sixties (at least). They all had big moustaches and gripped two or three cigarettes in each hand and were drooling over some hugely overweight women who looked completely bonkers. What the fuck was all that about?

"Pashto cinema," Sultan said. "Complete crap movies which rip out your heart and soul and burn your ears and feed to the dogs hanging from the trees between the porno shit with the devil." He unwound his window and spat into the street.

"I see," I said.

"Meanwhile, we are stuck," Palakorn said. "We're far too conspicuous."

I should point out that Palakorn went to Gordonstoun, the fancy but brutal Scottish school where Prince Charles and his father and a couple of other royals went and got the shit beaten out of them. Palakorn got kicked out for plotting to rearrange the face of one of the younger royals. The plan was that all his life, when the maimed royal appeared on the telly, he could tell whichever girl was in his bed at the time: "I did that."

"What should we do?" I asked. I mean, Palakorn did this sort of a thing for a living. He knew this stuff. He had been to wars and emerged without hating anyone who hadn't. He was very classy.

"We jump out," he said. "Sultan is safer without us."

"The driver will be safe," Sultan said. "You foreign shits fuck off and make me safe."

We jumped out of the car and were off, dodging and weaving in between crap cars and side stalls selling more of the same

DVD nonsense with the moustachioed old men. Palakorn led the way down a side street, where two old men were bent over and appeared to be strangling a cat, raising a lot of khaki dust. Within a minute we were in the back of a tiny, battered cab on another road and going another way.

There was a white arched sign "St John's Cathedral High School (English medium)", with high, red, brick walls each side and a grim two-storey building behind with its windows shuttered. There wasn't a child in sight. It didn't look like a busy hive of learning and play. Nearby was a "directorate of education – diocese of Peshawar, church of Pakistan" behind the same red brick wall, with blossom tumbling over the side. This was the town where the Taliban had targeted a high school run by the army and massacred 132 children in cold blood, going from classroom to classroom and shooting under the desks when the children tried to hide. How could anyone do that? Children. Soon we were in a hubbub of commercial activity, surrounded by garishly painted buses with shot tyres and grown men too big for the seats, their bare, sandaled feet at an uncomfortably high level, visible though the mud-spattered windows. They looked at us and scowled. One bus was painted with stylised Egyptian-style bird designs. One picture had "well come" written above it, another "super star". Then a bigger sign: "WAQASCOH" with "VIP" written underneath. Fuck knows what that was about.

A crowd had gathered at an intersection where dozens of electrical wires ran haphazardly overhead. There were the flags of Marina's party.

"I want to get out here," Palakorn said.

"Sure."

He squeezed out of his seat and disappeared into the crowd with his cameras. I paid off the cab.

"Where's the taxi?" Palakorn asked, coming back into view.

I glanced at the taxi crawling away through the crowd. "I thought…"

"Get him back! Tell him to wait for us. I don't want to be stuck here at sunset without a fucking beer. What were you thinking?"

"How…?"

"Tell him there's another hundred rupees in it if he waits. Tell him it could be an hour, it could be ten hours. He'll wait."

"Where?"

"Get his cell phone number. Tell him to stay central and we will call him. Hadley, what's the matter with you? This is basic stuff." Why was this man shouting at me? I was distracted, that was all. "Oh, forget the taxi," he said. "Come on, let's go."

We set off along the edge of the crowd, taxis and big political SUVs with darkened windows brushing us as they passed. Crowds seemed to be pressing in on us from all sides and suddenly police whistles were blowing. I was feeling a little disconsolate, to tell the truth. A bit uneasy. I was frowning and thought briefly about a large gin and tonic in an aeroplane plastic glass to cheer myself up. And there was of course the chance that I would see Marina sooner rather than later. Of course I would see her, and maybe I would get to talk to her. And this was just my first full day back in Pakistan. My heart leapt lightly.

"Hello again, Mister Hadley!" someone shouted. "Are you still with the press?"

Marina Makhdoom, leaning out the window of a Range Rover, was now talking to someone else who tried to put a garland around her neck and was beaten back by police for his efforts. Now she had an old man's hands in her hands and the crowd pushed nearer. I heard her say "bless you" twice in English. I looked at the long fingers, saw a heavy man's watch on her left wrist and heavy gold rings. The car was moving slowly and steadily forward, police hitting anyone who got in the way. Palakorn was close now, snapping away within two feet of her face. I pushed nearer.

"Jump in," she said.

"Really?" I caught Palakorn's eye.

"Please embark. You can interview me. We'll soon be done here." She turned and gave instructions in Urdu to her aides.

"Can my photographer come?"

"Of course. The more the merrier."

This was too good to be true. There were beads of sweat on Marina's forehead and her lipstick was gently smudged. We climbed into the back, with minders either side. The doors slammed shut, drowning out the mass worshippers outside. The windows closed with a hum and there was air-conditioned silence. Marina turned and smiled.

"Are you sitting most comfortably?"

"Most comfortably," I said, watching the crowd part in front of us, a strangely wild look in the eyes of two boys who spread red bauhinia petals over the bonnet.

"Where is your usual reporter?" Marina asked. "The Shrubs bureau chief?"

"He's out meeting sources."

"I see. So we are going to drive away from here, stopping along the way to speak to my loyal and long-suffering supporters," Marina said. "To give them succour and hope. Nothing too exhausting. You want to ask me questions as we drive?"

"That would be great, thanks." Succour and hope? Was she taking the piss?

"I remember you from Hong Kong," she added.

"I remember too," I said. Lordy, lordy.

"Yes. I seem to recall you saying you didn't travel much in your job. And yet here you are in Pakistan. With your handsome photographer."

"I am flattered you remember," I said. "I have always treasured my visits to Pakistan." Treasured? Why did she say Palakorn was handsome?

"I am happy to hear that," she said. "And if the current government would spend less time lining its pockets with the people's money and spend a little more on roads, education, hospitals and other desperately needed infrastructure, the visits could be even more of a treasure, I believe."

"I hear you," I said. And yet my hearing had never been in question. She wasn't a doctor. I liked the way she pronounced "government" "gow-ment". It was a simple flaw, a reminder that she was human and talking to me. "Perhaps you could tell me your plans," I said. "If you get elected, I mean."

I pulled out my recorder, switched it on and turned my notebook to a new page. At the top I wrote Marina's name, with a big tick next to it signifying very little at this stage. I usually reserved ticks for usable quotes.

"Can you be a bit more specific?" she asked.

"What would be your top priority?"

"Definitely easing the predicament and struggle of the rural poor."

"Ah," I said. I managed to stop myself saying "nice one".

"I think there would be no exaggeration in my speech if I said the poor in Pakistan, in the towns and the villages, have been oppressed for far too long. It is time that the shackles of feudalism and servitude are severed at last."

"How would you go about that?"

"That's a good and important question. I think it all comes down to education and a will on the part of the government to change perceptions."

"Right. Let me throw your question to me back at you: can you be more specific?"

Marina smiled. "I see you believe in a tough line of questioning. I like that."

"Thanks." Why was I thanking her? I was asking ball-achingly stupid, pathetic questions and she was talking total bollocks. Palakorn was taking pictures in a blur of clicks every time she turned her head.

"It's a matter of seizing the moment, of grasping the nettle and saying 'I am not letting go until the pain is gone'," she said.

"After addressing poverty and enslavement, I would turn my attention to health care and the economy."

"Right."

"But not necessarily in that order."

"Oh, right."

"I don't want you pinning me down on my policy platform before I have even been elected."

Ha ha. I stopped pretending to take notes. I looked her in her sparkling eye as some poor sod got his head stowed in against the driver's door and sank to the ground. Was she being serious? Did she think anyone with half a mind would buy this stuff?

There was an explosion over the trees, but not big enough to distract the crowd for long. Bombs in Peshawar were not rare. Without saying a word, Palakorn jumped out of the car and headed in the direction of the blast. The two aides got out too, leaving me, Marina and the driver.

"I think we should leave," she said. "Will your handsome friend be all right?"

"I ought to go with him."

"But this is nothing. A small scare. And I am a good source, am I not? My driver does not speak any English. At some point in the interview, would you like to talk about other things?"

"Other things?"

She was coming on to me. And Palakorn was out there. And I was in here. And...

"Do you have enough information for your story?" she asked.

"Not really, but that isn't important." My heart was beating fast. She smiled and turned to face the crowd in front. She pointed ahead and she and the driver exchanged a few words, presumably deciding our escape route.

"You know where we are, of course?" she said, turning back to me. "You know how dangerous it is for you here? Even more for you than me."

"Yes," I said.

"We are going to head back to Islamabad, is that okay?"

"Yes. Can I ask another question?"

"Of course."

"Why is there so much violence in Pakistan? Why are there so many assassinations and bombs?"

"I assume you are talking about political violence, not the insurgency."

"Yes, the politics."

"Because this is Pakistan," she said, turning to the driver and giving further instructions in Urdu. She turned back. Her eyes were the kind that a fully veiled woman, showing nothing but her eyes, could be killed for. "We have our ways of doing things. It is so easy, so felicitous, for many people in the West to say 'oh, Pakistani politics is so corrupt and violent', as if there wasn't one well-intentioned, good fellow among us. But you are mistaken. You think my father is not a good man? You think I am a wicked woman? One person cannot change a country's political history. You have to work with it, realise its strengths and its weaknesses, its good intentions and wicked ways. It means we must all sometimes resort to wicked ways. Or we would all be killed."

"Have you been wicked?" I asked. "I mean, have you ever ordered someone to be killed, for instance?" I said, making clear that I didn't expect a serious answer. She didn't answer. "Has anyone tried to kill you?"

"There are rumours of plots all the time," she said. "There are rumours that my dear husband wants to kill me. By the way, this is all between us."

"Of course."

"I don't even know why I am telling you, but I feel I can trust you after what happened in Hong Kong."

"Yes, you can trust me. I won't breathe a word." I was a fatuous prick.

"We all have our sources of information," she said. "The conjuring trick is to act on that which is credible, on the legitimate concerns, and not to be gullible. It is something of which we are all aware. Would you like to go to a bar with me?"

"So sorry, didn't quite catch the last bit?"

"Would you like to go to a bar? I am going to take you to a bar. Would that be agreeable to you?"

"I'd have to think that one over."

"Ah, you are being ironic. Is that right?"

"I am being sarcastic. I would love to go to a bar with you."

"That is first class."

CHAPTER FOUR

ISLAMABAD WAS DESIGNED by Greek architects in the 1950s and built at the foot of the majestic Margalla Hills. It is a green city built on a grid system with glorious, leafy, half-tended streets of large houses with large gardens with big expanses of lawn, each with one or two guards whose main job was to open and close heavy metal gates behind coming and going four-wheel drives. Inside the houses, many, as I said, ugly from the outside, the rooms have high ceilings, unwieldy furniture and electrical fittings that look like they were made in the 1930s. Now, in the late spring, the evenings were cool and there was an autumn-like mist as crows cawed from high, white-painted brick walls between the gardens before flying into the tall trees, or to the edges of construction skips full of fetid waste.

Marina's car turned into one of these wooded streets, a cul de sac, and at the end turned into a drive, the gate opening automatically. The car doors were opened from the outside and the door to the bar opened at the same time. We were swept in by silent men in dark suits looking over our heads towards the road. I followed Marina down a spiral, metal staircase into what looked like an Italian restaurant in Bloomsbury, a small room with red velvet walls and small round tables, a bar along one wall where a white barman, dressed in white, was waiting and smiling. There were no other guests. Marina said a few words and the security men and aides left us.

"Please wait one moment," she told me. "Order yourself a

drink."

"Can I get you something?"

"He knows."

She left through a door next to the bar. I nodded to the barman and studied the pictures along the wall next to the drinks, pictures of army generals, smiling politicians, and one of Marina with her father greeting some Westerner I didn't recognise. I ordered a Pakistan-made Sparkhayes beer. A big silent screen was showing cricket on the wall opposite the bar.

"Monsieur?" the barman said. "You are sure that you would like to experiment with the local beer?"

"If it's not too much trouble."

"No trouble at all, sir. It is a fine beer. But be – how do you say in English – abstemious. Not too much."

"Don't worry, I can hold my drink."

"That is not my deepest fear, monsieur."

"I'm sorry?"

"Please, I apologise if I am teaching a grandmother how to fuck eggs. But does it not appear a little strange to you that a country that disallows alcohol in public makes its own beer and spirits?"

"Suck eggs."

"Monsieur?"

"The expression. Teach your grandmother to suck eggs. Not fuck eggs."

"But I was having a little joke," he said. "I was having a jape with the English language. It was obviously not very successful."

He wore a white jacket, white tie and white waistcoat over tight white flannels. "It's not very successful," I said, "because no one in their right mind would teach their grandmother to fuck anything, let alone half a dozen freshly laid eggs." I didn't want to be too hard on him. "Are you French?"

"Monsieur is very perceptive, I believe. Please partake of my word – do not drink too much of the beer."

"Why not?"

"The company will deny the use of glycerine. Without attempting another joke, I must say that after about six cans, your bowels will open as if by detonation. No one will be safe for yards around."

"Good grief."

"I'll bring your drinks."

My phone went. I could hear the shouting before I had raised it to my ear. I had completely forgotten about Palakorn.

"You leave me in the fucking middle of nowhere, you don't call, you fuck off with that fucking woman. What the fuck do you think you are doing?"

"Palakorn, I am so sorry."

"I mean, a bomb goes off. And you *fuck* off and leave me in the middle of fucking nowhere. How unprofessional is that?"

"I thought you'd be okay. She wanted to go somewhere."

"She wanted to go somewhere? I was in the middle of fucking nowhere!"

"I was going to circle back."

"Circle back? What are you, a boomerang? Some sort of fucking homing pigeon?"

"Are you all right? Was it a big bomb?"

"It was nothing."

"Where are you?"

"I'm at the Pearl-Continental."

"Well, that's nice."

"Well it is now. No thanks to you. I mean where in the hostile training manual does it say if there's a bomb, and your colleague has gone to investigate, you should turn the car around and take off at speed, pebbles spitting from under the wheels?"

"What can I say? You're so macho. And she turned my head."

Palakorn hung up and my phone rang again immediately. Number unknown.

"Hello?"

"Hello. Be."

"Sorry?"

"Hello. Be. My."

"Who is this?"

"Hello. Be. My. Servan-ter."

"Oh for fuck's sake."

I hung up. This was getting creepy.

The beer came. I'd had it before many times and the barman didn't know what he was talking about. I knocked it back in one, banged the glass on the bar top and signalled for another.

My phone went again. Gary's number.

"Hey, man," I said.

"Hey, Hadley. Just wanted to say how sorry I am I couldn't be on your trip to Peshawar. How did things go?"

"Good," I said. "They went well. I got to speak to Marina."

There was a pause. "You got to speak to Marina?"

"Yes. Palakorn was there. She picked us up in her car. We should have a great story."

Another pause. "I've never got to speak to Marina," he said.

"Well, it wasn't difficult. We were in the street..."

"Hadley?"

"Yes, Gary?"

"Shut it."

Gary hung up. What the fuck? I didn't have time to think about it. Marina reappeared. She had changed into a loose, dark green, silk curtain-like affair that billowed at the top and grasped her ankles at the bottom. She had freshened her lipstick. I stood up as she took her seat and took a sip of her gin and tonic. The barman brought my beer.

"You must be wondering why I have invited you here," she said.

"I feel honoured."

"Well there's no need. That is the point. I wanted to see you again as two normal people having refreshment, and this is where it is possible."

"Who runs the place? I have been in other bars in Islamabad, but this is the most discreet."

"The military runs it, believe it or not. It is not common knowledge. But I feel I already know you well enough to know that you won't share my little secret."

"Of course, I won't."

"And perhaps we could meet here again."

"I would like that."

"How's the beer?"

"It's cold and delicious. Tell me, Mrs …"

"Please call me Marina."

"Marina. Do other people come here?"

"Of course."

"Other famous politicians?"

"Yes, one or two. But they are all friends. I hope. Barring all the information I was giving you in the car. Off the record."

"Of course. But won't people mind you telling me about the place?"

"You will not divulge the information." She reached into her bag and pulled out a gun.

"Whoa."

"Hadley, it's okay. Relax. You know what this is?"

I looked around. "It's a gun. Why have you pulled out a gun?"

"Don't worry. This is a place I can do what I like and get away with it. It's a silver pistol. It's for my protection. I also have a knife."

She delved into the bag and brought out a knife which she unsheathed in a swift move. "This is a twelve-inch Bowie knife."

"As opposed to a twelve-inch Bowie single." She didn't appear to hear me.

"And I save the best for last." She replaced the weapons and brought what looked like a child's pencil case, with a zip running along the top. She opened the zip slowly and delicately brought out the largest spliff I had ever seen. It was the shape and size of a pipe bomb.

"This is how I get off," she said. "I want to suck on this mother right now. Like sucking an exhaust pipe on an automobile, you know what I mean? My mouth open wide. Stretching my lips. I want to draw on this to the maximum effect, to take it in and hold it there so I cannot speak. Do you ever experience that sensation?"

Borderline crazy, I reckoned. "Marina, are you sure it's okay to do this? Here, I mean?"

To give you an idea how big this joint was, she used half a toilet roll as a roach. There was also a no-smoking zone sign on the wall, which didn't carry much weight when we were drinking in a no-drinking country.

"Your chest starts to heave with pleasure," she said. "And your abdomen. You start to look at things in a different way. You see a dog and the dog looks at you and you think: Can you read my thoughts? Like, are you god?"

"Big departure from Islam, then."

She lit the spliff with a candle on the table, rolling the flame round and around, and took one of those big intakes of breath which make you speak like you're being strangled underwater.

"Big time. Departure. Like a gleaming airport departure hall. Jesus."

"In another town. Dubai, perhaps. Bangkok."

"Fuck me this is good stuff."

"And another question: does your husband ever come here?"

"Husband?"

"Yes."

"You want a hit?"

"No thanks. I don't really feel in the mood."

"You think I am going to call the police?" She took another hit and spoke to me as if through a voice box being fed too much electricity. "You remember what I was saying about rumours my husband wanted to kill me?"

"Marina, please, not so loud."

She paid no attention. "I actually and specifically told him. I told him that if I found out that he was plotting to kill me, I would plot to kill him first."

"It sounds like two senators conspiring in Ancient Rome. Underneath the arches of the Coliseum."

"It would be touch and go who would get to whom first." She inhaled again and this time spoke in a high-pitched, barely audible wheeze: "I told him... during the... conjugal proceedings."

"Oh wow."

"The look... on his face... was a spectacularly magic moment... for both of us. First class."

I had to turn this conversation back to the subject of murder. I didn't want to hear about any more magic moments.

"Why would he want to kill you?"

"He has his political ambitions too. And yet I am the people's favourite, despite my faith. I will be the next prime minister. What more efficacious than to kill me and win all my supporters by default in sympathy? But of course he would have to make sure that the finger of blame for my killing was directed at his and my opponents. That would necessarily be the case. The people here are very poorly educated. They would not suspect such a Machiavellian plot. They would support him."

"Good grief."

"Or he could get jealous. It is no secret that I have had paramours. My husband and I have an understanding."

"Ah." Again I managed not to say "nice one".

She took a big hit and addressed me, sounding like Donald Duck locked in an ice-box. "The men could be a bit of a political embarrassment."

"I can imagine that."

Another fast intake of smoke and then in a soprano gasp: "But that's where the Christianity helps. As a Muslim woman,

I would stand no chance. As a Christian, I have already been written off by a large section of the population as a heretic. In that respect, I have god on my side."

"You were talking about your husband."

"He does not come here. But he knows I do. He is cognisant of many things. I am sure he knows I am here with you contemporaneously. He will listen to your conversations in all sorts of unexpected places with nefarious designs." I thought of the pictures of the small man with the big gun and his posse of bodyguards. "He has his own places where he goes, where I don't go, but where many young and beautiful women go too. Do you understand what I am saying?"

"I do."

"Many of these beautiful young woman are English. Does that surprise you? Don't get me wrong. I love my husband and he loves me. But we are ambitious people. We are like business partners. He is very powerful. He is a lusty and lascivious man. He needs his releases."

I couldn't help feel a little turned on. I don't know if it was the glycerine-free Sparkhayes, the smoke from the haystack in her mouth, or the open, easy suggestions of decadent deception from one of the most beautiful faces in front of me, candlelight on moist lips.

"Marina."

"What is it?"

"Do you, by any chance, want to ..."

"Want to what?"

"Well, go somewhere."

"Go somewhere? Why would I want to go somewhere now?"

Did I really have to spell it out? "Go somewhere else," I said.

"Go somewhere else?"

"Well, yes."

"Stop there, Hadley. Hold your horse. I ought to warn you about the kind of company my husband keeps."

"You mean… the women?"

"No, not the women. His security team. Just take my word. Don't ever give them cause for suspicion."

"I see. Thank you."

"For a woman, it takes time to feel that way about a man. But that is alongside the point. Watch out for one who wears cotton wool in his ears."

"Cotton wool?"

"He seems very friendly, but he is a mean, mean man. I don't have to go any further, I hope."

"He has an infection?"

"He has a disease. Any sharp noise puts him to sleep. Instantaneously."

"So in case there is any car backfiring…"

"Or gunshot. Or improvised explosive device. That is the reason."

"Wow. I shall forever be looking in men's ears."

"That is not all."

"His adenoids?"

She looked briefly at the ceiling. "This man is violent in the degree of infinity. He has depraved appetites."

I downed my beer and the barman was there immediately at my shoulder with another can. What was that look on his face? Defiance? I'd show him.

Marina's phone rang. She pushed back her hair and an ear ring shaped like a chandelier. "Tikka," she said. Then after a long pause: "Tikka… Ah-cha. Ah-cha… Tikka." She hung up.

"I am afraid I am going to have to leave now, by myself," she said. "I have an appointment I cannot ignore. I want you to stay here a while. Is that all right?"

"Yes. Thank you for having me. I hope everything is okay?"

"Yes, everything is first class. I had a wonderful time. Next time perhaps we shall dance to Spanish music. The bill is not a matter of your or my concern."

"You are most kind."

She touched my hand and did that thing with her fingers and was off up the spiral staircase, her bangles clattering gently against the iron banister.

I HAD HAD NINE BEERS by the time I left, giving Cyrano de Bergerac a knowing smile and pulling myself up the stairs and into the long drive down to the road. Okay, I was a bit tipsy but that was all. Explosions like there was no tomorrow?

"My arse," I said.

The guard let me out through the tall metal gate and my plan had been to walk down to the main road and jump into one of the minuscule gas-fired taxis whose large drivers looked like goats penned into rabbit cages. A man wearing a dark shalwar kameez approached from behind. He had come from a battered old car with three friends all looking out the window at me. The man was about forty-five and wore sparkly ear rings. I like Islamabad and feel safe. But my first thought this time was that if some insurgent group wanted to kidnap me, a Shrubs journalist, what better plan than to send a man wearing diamonds in his ears and a bunch of mates for back-up when I was a bit pissed? Then I remembered. It was the solemn man I had seen in Rick's Cafe back in Hong Kong.

"Eh-up," the man said.

"I'm sorry?"

"Is this the guesthouse?"

"The guesthouse." Think quickly, Hadley. Just don't mention the booze. Why the Yorkshire accent?

"No guesthouse," I said. "Just a restaurant."

"A restaurant, you say." He was eyeing me up and down. I did not feel relaxed. I was expecting a line like: "Int' back 't' car. Now. In fact, int' boot."

"Is this the place where they do the massages?" he said.

"Massages?"

"Aye, lad. Massages. Me and me mates fancy a roob."

He turned briefly to the car to signal his mates.

"A roob?"

"Aye. A good roob. My name's Todd and I fancy a bit of 'ankeh-pankeh."

"I think you may have the wrong place." Trooble down't massage parlour.

"Oh, I could have sworn that this were the place, like. So where are you from?"

"I live in Hong Kong."

"You don't look Chinese."

"No, I'm not. I'm from England. But I live in Hong Kong."

"You don't say. I'm from Leeds. I used to sell cars. What do you do?"

"I'm a journalist." I shouldn't have said that, of course. I don't know why I made such a basic error in what many people still considered a hostile environment. If there was any time to get "int' boot", this was it. But it wasn't. "All I want to write about is tea."

"What?"

"That is my dream. To write about tea."

"But we don't grow tea in Pakistan. Well, we tried once, back in the day, like. But the soil and climatic conditions were not right, you see. I know this for a fact. They weren't conducive."

"What I mean is, I would like to write about that. The possibilities. Of trying to grow tea in Pakistan again."

"Oh right. Well it's been a pleasure to speak to you," Todd said. "Me and me mates will be off then."

"Okay."

"If there's no 'ankeh-pankeh, there's no 'ankeh-pankeh."

"There's no hanky-panky, as far as I know."

"We'll just have to take your word for it."

"Aye."

He walked back to the car and turned. "A real nice pleasure

talking to you, 'Ad-leh."

"You too. Wait. How do you know my name?"

"I'm Todd, by the way. Yorkshire Todd. We drink lots of tea in Yorkshire. Brick red, it is."

He and his mates stared at me as the car took off along the street. Only he was smiling. The others looked ready to kill.

CHAPTER FIVE

THE FIRST STOP the next day was the Supreme Court to hear a blasphemy case against a former military leader and friend of Marina's dad who was also a closet Christian. No verdict was expected, but I just wanted to see what the place looked and felt like. A bit of what we in the trade call "colour" for the story about the world stacked up against Marina and her political career. I still hadn't been to the office yet. And I hadn't managed to reconnect with Gary the bureau chief. His phone was permanently off. What a strange way to run an operation. Blasphemy, as it happens, carries the death penalty in Pakistan. But anyone who says their religious feelings have been injured can bring a case. And it's tough to get a lawyer to defend you, because he could be accused of blasphemy too, just by being on your side. The lawyers get shot dead in the street outside the courts and the people who do the shooting are hailed, by some, as heroes. There are people banged up in jail across the country on trumped up charges. It is a bizarre and hugely corrupt system.

I sat in the press box for over an hour and nothing noticeable happened. So much grandeur, so much gravitas, so little progress. All men, of course. I wondered why the lawyer in front of me, in a dark suit turning to green mould, was shaking his leg so violently. It was as annoying as a flickering neon light.

The Supreme Court is bright, dramatic and splendid from the outside. It's a dark, dull and poorly maintained maze on the inside. Court One is about a hundred feet tall and bathed in a weird yellow light through triangular windows in the ceiling which gives the cheap, brown veneered woodwork below a psychedelic orange tinge. There is room for up to twenty judges and there's seating for about two hundred. The walls are covered with portraits of old judges in wigs. There are ancient law books everywhere and I bet no one had looked at one of them in years. The one I could see nearest the press box was "The Journal and Supreme Court: PLD 1" and dated 1964. The title didn't make sense. Nor, I dared wager, did the contents. Who needs a 1964 law book? No one. It just looked the part, someone thought. Fusty, pompous and useless.

There were two lines of lawyers wearing the same black suits and cheap leather shoes, all about seventy and all dusty and half dead. In front of them were clerks sifting through pile after pile of papers, folders and files, about two feet tall and tied up with string (the piles, not the clerks). They looked like stacks of newspapers and people kept on bringing in more on their shoulders. One man was holding a pot of glue. Who was going to get around to reading that lot? About the same number who would get around to reading 1964 law books about four inches thick. Was it vital evidence? Why wasn't it slimmed down and online? Or chucked it into the nearest skip? How many lives were going to be well and truly screwed over just because no one in the room cared?

And then the violence began. It was like a runaway train made of milk smashing into the back of stationary train made of rubber in a tunnel which had a door I managed to close just in time. It was an enormous and terrifying shock and I made a short, loud "woo" noise. A bit like a train, in fact. Good grief, it was sudden. I tried not to think about it. Lots of people were filling the public gallery now, looking towards the stage, hoping for words of wisdom, and one reporter sat next to me and he also started shaking his leg. I was furious. Being furious was one thing. But being furious and urgently having to go to the lav was another. Why had it only taken hold now? I had been fine that morning. I was out of my seat and marching along the orange carpet towards the exit. I kept my legs straight and my buttocks clenched. I imagined I looked like a World War Two air force veteran with wooden legs. I imagined I looked like I had a pool cue up my arse. I could have done with a pool cue up my arse, to tell you the truth. The pressure, the pressure.

"Eh-up. Soomwoon's in a hoo-reh." Oh lord. It was Yorkshire Todd. He was sitting in the audience. In an aisle seat. What was he doing there?

"No," I said. "Please. Not now."

"I might as well tell ya. I foond a good roob."

"Please let me go. How did you know my name?"

"No, I mean I found a right good massage."

"No, no."

"Aye. A real Yorkshire toob."

A Yorkshire toob. I didn't know what he was on about and I didn't care. I was out in the marble corridor within seconds and in the men's room downstairs in seconds more, brushing aside a security guard.

"Gentleman, you cannot use the facility," he said.

"What do you mean?" There was no could or couldn't about it. I had to.

"There is no facility."

"What?" I opened the door to the only lav going and there was nothing inside. Nothing.

"There is no shit hole," the guard said.

"So what do I do?" I tried to keep my voice low.

"You leave the court, cross the hallway, down the passage, rise the stairs…"

"Rise the stairs? Wait…"

"…turn left at the marble flowers and behove yourself to the left. There you can take a taxi…"

"A taxi?" My voice was a high alto. Take a taxi? Are you

fucking joking? I was about to behove myself right there and then. This man did not understand the urgency. The impending crisis. "What are you saying? I need to go to the bathroom, not the airport. Don't you have a bathroom that works?"

"Before the taxi stand is my meaning. There you can find a stationary and portable toilet."

It wasn't going to move then. "Terrific. Many thanks."

This was going to be very close and I had to run. Or jog, at least. I started off, my shoulders heaving from side to side in a big arc. I trotted away, keeping my knees as close together as possible. If only I could be scared shitless again, as in the guesthouse. I tried to console myself by thinking that whatever happens now, one day I will laugh about it over a beer. Except don't think of the beer! Don't think of that nitro-glycerine still swishing around your bowels, leaving record high-water marks.

There were the marble flowers. I behove myself to the left and there it was. One lav in a tiny Nissen hut. A squat toilet. I ripped open the door and my belt like a magician unveiling something magical. I ripped my trousers down over my knees, squatted and… fuck me the release! The overwhelming relief. And with the relief, the overwhelming stench! It was alien! Someone outside bellowed in Urdu, almost bringing the house down. I don't speak Urdu, but I suspect he was saying something along the lines of: *"Rescue me! For all that is precious and dear to me, what the fuck is that smell?"*

The humiliation. There came a horrible, screaming, wail, from further away, along the tones of: *how is this possible? From what planet does this smell emanate? If I go anywhere near that room I will surely die.* And to add to my despair, there was no paper. Just a small water jug. That wasn't going to do the trick. Not even close. And there was all that absorbent paper in the courtroom and that made me even more furious. I looked at the pot of water again. It was like a teapot.

I checked my pockets. No tissues, no hanky, no hanky-panky,

that was for sure, just a fancier-than-usual notebook with hard, shiny paper as absorbent as steel. This would not do. I don't want to go on. I'm not going to go into details. Suffice it to say I left that godforsaken place with no notebook and the cleaner, when he eventually dared enter after tracking down chemical-gas-protective clothing and a mask, would have seen a pyramid of paper in the corner and said in Urdu the equivalent of: *Sweet. Baby. James.*

I RETURNED TO THE GUESTHOUSE to shower and looked forward to a large gulp from the bottle in my case.

"Ah, you have interrupted your work day to come back to see men at work?"

The manager was behind the counter and his mates were sitting in the same seats. Where were the women? What were they doing? Another productive day in Islamabad.

"Yes, hi," I said. "I've come back for a shower." Why I felt the need to give them an explanation was beyond me.

"That's great, sir," the manager said. "We are here should you need anything more. Anything in the way of refreshment?"

"No, thanks. I am fine."

"Thank you, sir."

But I wasn't fine. I felt awful. The scotch didn't help at all. I felt so bad that I suspected I had a bout of food-poisoning. Nothing to do with the Sparkhayes at all. I lay on my bed and slept, only to wake in the middle of the night. I was feverish and lonely. It is the only time I feel lonely – when I am sick and realise no one knows or can do anything about it. I looked at my watch. It was nothing like the middle of the night. It was one in the morning. I had hours of this shit before I could call the office and say I would take the day off.

And then the banging noises began again. I could not lift myself off the bed. I dozed and woke and dozed and dreamt. I was too sick to be scared. I woke again when the kettle was hissing at its highest.

The next day I had a light breakfast of toast and coffee delivered to the room and slept again.

"The night, sir," the waiter said. "Was it more peaceful?"

I didn't have any energy. "No, not at all. I'm sorry. I'm tired and don't feel very well," I said.

I slept all day. I woke in the evening feeling enlivened and took a quick slug of scotch. Yes. The guesthouse was a five-minute walk from the Kohsar market, a friendly shopping area popular with expats with an excellent English-language bookshop and good coffee, backing on to the big gardens of houses where diplomats and journalists lived. I would eat there and see how I felt.

I showered and changed and stepped outside the guesthouse, waiting for the guard in his box to put down his tea and open the gate to the street. I could have easily done it myself and it would have been much quicker, but then the guard would have nothing to do all day. Outside on Aga Khan Road, where pretty purple flowers dotted the grass between the two double lanes, a line of the same tiny taxis was waiting, their burly drivers with their big heads looking at me balefully. It's not my fault you drive cars which are fifteen times too small for you, I wanted to say. It's not my fault that life for some people is shit. Two men on the pavement came up from each side and asked if I wanted a taxi. I explained that I just wanted to walk up to Kohsar market to get some food and look at the books.

"That is a long walk," one said.

"It's five, ten minutes at the most," I said.

"Ten minutes. In this climate?"

I didn't know what kind of climate he was talking about, but the evening was mild, a light, ice-crystal cirrostratus cloud formation covering the sun. It was heavenly.

I started northwest up Street 14 and was crossing the road by a modest-looking Sony centre when one of the tiny taxis pulled up alongside me. It was one of the baleful men.

"You get in, Mister Englishman."

"No, thanks. I want to walk."

"No, thanks, Mister Englishman. You get in." I ignored him and kept walking and he followed along the kerb. "You want pretty girl?" he asked.

Hang on a minute. No one had ever propositioned me like that in Islamabad. And if they had, I would have been worried. I was worried.

"What?"

"There's a place."

Oh, there's a place, is there? "I just want to walk," I said politely. After all, this could have been some Islamist militant with a big knife in his dashboard. At least a knife that could fit in the dashboard of the tiny car, a Suzuki Mehran, a whining, lawn-mower with a flat, angular 1970s design I had only ever seen in Pakistan. It was black with a lime-yellow roof.

I kept on walking, faster now, a high, white wall to my left overhung by shooting twigs of a bush the other side which caught my hair. The driver changed down to second with a crunch and a curse and leapt twenty yards up the road and stopped. The big man climbed out, walked round the front of the car and on to the pavement and stood his ground.

"Get in the car, please, Mister Englishman. There's a place with girls."

"Well, so you keep saying. What kind of place?"

"You can drink, you can dance. I get commission. You will like."

It was a lovely evening and I was feeling much better. I could have done with some food first, but...

"I'll give it a shot," I said. "You'd better not be messing me around."

The man patted the roof of his car once and hard, as if to say: Gotcha.

We drove on to the Margalla Road, dodging a herd of goats, past the cricket ground and jogging track and past Marina's home. I couldn't see any sign of life in the upper windows, the only ones visible over the high wall.

"Marina Makhdoom home," the driver said.

"Yes."

"I also Christian." The driver showed me the cross around his neck in the mirror. "*Thy will be done as it is in heaven.* You will like pretty girls."

We turned left at the giant mosque at the foot of the hills, then into a series of turns in and out of leafy avenues. The driver stopped.

"You get out here please. I don't have time."

Say what? The giant kidnaps me, drives me halfway across the city to some alleged bar and then tells me he doesn't have the time?

"This is great. You want me to walk to my destination? You're a taxi driver, but you don't have time to drive your taxi?"

"It is over there," he said. "Right side. By that big tree with the larks. It's the Korean restaurant and golf shop. On dead leafy street."

I could see a big tree, but larks? I paid him two hundred rupees and he did a fast, noisy three-point-turn and sped back the way he had come, leaving a cloud of totally unsexy-smelling burnt compressed natural gas in the air. I walked up the silent, dirt driveway next to the big tree. There was no restaurant sign but there was a bag of golf clubs propped up against the wall next to the front door. I had that incredibly familiar and welcome sensation in the chest before entering a house of fun. My heart was bubbling.

I knocked. The door opened and another giant of a man bowed to greet me.

"Is this the Korean restaurant?" I asked.

The man stepped back and bowed again and ushered me in

with his arm. He didn't answer my question. Bizarre.

"You are most welcome," he said at last.

Next to him, in a line, were three middle-aged women all dressed up in flowering saris and bangles and gold, all smiling at me, their hands held out to greet a Westerner none of them had seen before. I glanced into the huge room with big, building-like furniture, dark wallpaper, naff chandelier and heavy drawn curtains. There were about ten old women sitting on sofas looking at me through their glasses, smiling and frowning at the same time. I went down the line shaking hands.

"Hello, I'm Hadley. Hello, I'm Hadley. Hello..." It dawned on me that there might have been a mistake. This was some sort of family gathering. A fiftieth wedding anniversary perhaps. Or could it have been a funeral and they were just being too gracious to tell me to fuck off and leave them alone in their grief?

"This isn't a Korean restaurant," I said to the room.

No one disagreed. No one said a thing.

The man who had ushered me in clapped his hands. The old women climbed stiffly out of their enormous sofas and shuffled past me through high double doors to the back of the house.

"Come along, come along, you crumbly old women," the man said. "Don't be a dawdling."

Don't be a dawdling was it now? What a rude man. And now the room was emptying, the three old maids in a row had vanished and the man was walking backwards, pulling the double doors to behind him. I was all alone.

"Please don't leave me," I said to no one, mock-theatrically you understand. "Not in this big spooky house."

"But you are not alone, Hadley."

I turned quickly. Marina was standing at the double doors. She was wearing a shalwar kameez over jeans, her hair done up in a bun.

"Oh my word," I said.

"Oh my word. I like that."

"You do?"

"It says a lot about you."

"It does?" She was walking towards me.

"You, as a man, are not so attractive. In looks, I mean. But you have this way about you that excises the self-conscious pretence."

"Wow." What was she talking about?

"I noticed it the first night I met you. It was just a look, but it spoke volumes. A certain innocence."

I couldn't help thinking that if I played my cards right, this innocent was in here. What was going on?

"Have you any idea how attractive a liberal Western man is, no matter how ugly, to a Christian woman from a conservative Pakistan family? It is literally magnetic. It is an exciting opportunity to break free."

"Marina." What was I going to say? I was at a loss for words. "You want to break free?"

"The lord knows."

"I am sorry, Marina, I am totally confused."

"I am so sorry. I am sure you will be especially wanting to know where you are and why you are here."

"Yes, I would like to know that."

"I told you before, Hadley. There are networks of security and intelligence. And of course not just in Hong Kong."

"But the taxi. The driver..."

"He used a line we thought would make you get in the car."

"We?"

"I have a team."

"And what made you think I would fall for the bait?"

"Don't be so foolish. That is the most innocent part."

"And what about all these people in the house?"

"This is their abode. They welcomed you in. I have an apartment in the rear quarters where we shall go now if you like. I have alcohol. Would you like to see my rear quarters? Would you like some alcohol?"

"Well, yes, I suppose I would. I wouldn't mind something to eat first though. A Marmite sandwich or something."

"A Marmite sandwich? My, how British. There shall be ample opportunity for disparate refreshments." She looked around to make sure everyone had gone. "I also have this." She rummaged in her bag and pulled out one of her industrial-piping-sized spliffs. "Perhaps today you will be in the mood."

She turned on her heels. I followed Marina through the tall double doors into a hall with a large table in the middle, a dark kitchen off to the right, with a refrigerator that looked like a small, upended caravan with rounded edges. Marina saw something to the left, gasped, stopped in her tracks and put her right hand across her heart.

An old man was leaning against the lowest stair banister, his hair quaffed back, his arm extended up the steep balustrade, a packet of Gauloises in his hand along with a gold lighter, a smile on his face which wobbled up and down as he chewed whatever he was chewing. He was wearing sunglasses in his hair and a grey suit over a stylish, cotton white shirt with no collar or tie. I thought it must be the golf pro or someone I could nod to and Marina and I would be on our way to smoke that enormous joint and get super-friendly. But I realised I knew the man. It took a few seconds before I realised I was standing in front of Mian Langhari, the same Mian Langhari the daft crop circle people had spotted with Marina in Hong Kong. He once scored a double century at Lord's and I had been there to see it! That was about thirty-five years ago. He was way too old for Marina, anyway. Surely. But he was, still was, very good looking. He was sneering at me. I resisted the urge to take out my notebook and ask for an autograph.

"Marina."

That was all he said in a husky, deep voice. The voice, actually, of a man with emphysema. He casually pushed himself up from the banister and walked past me in the direction Marina and I had been headed. What was going on? This was so unfair. He was wearing a powerful, exotic perfume which for some reason made me think of the pyramids. He opened a door, walked into another dark room without so much as a glance back at us and closed the door behind him. I looked at Marina. She still had her hand over her heart and was looking towards the door Mian Langhari had just ambled through like a fucking Egyptian cat. What was she doing? What was the look on her face? Terror? Huge disappointment? Love? Overwhelming lust? What did he have over her?

"Marina?"

That was all I said. My voice lacked Langhari's total command, but at least it didn't bubble with phlegm.

"I'm so sorry," she said.

"Why? I mean, why is he here? Do you have a date?" She was still looking at the door. "Marina?"

"I'm sorry, you will have to go."

"Go?"

"Yes. I had forgotten. I had an appointment. A date. I have to go. Extremely regrettable planning. I am so sorry. You can try the kitchen for your sandwich."

I realised then, for the first time, that I felt something other than the thrill of talking to, being with, someone beautiful and famous. It wasn't pleasant.

"Don't worry about the sandwich," I said.

"Yes," she said, still looking at the door.

"I mean, it's Mian Langhari, for heaven's sake." His perfume was stinking the whole place out. "I think he may have just bowled a maiden over."

"He's a famous cricketer."

My little joke went down well. Not! Boy oh boy, she was transfixed.

"Don't worry, Marina," I said. "I can see my own way out."

"Yes, yes, thanks. Eternally grateful. Bread in the bread bin.

Next to the Goblin Teasmade."

She walked slowly to the door, Mian Langhari no doubt leaning against something appropriate on the other side, maybe still with an article of clothing on. A sock, perhaps. Or a batsman's glove. On the end of his dick. She walked in and closed the door gently after her without so much as a farewell smile in my direction.

It did briefly occur to me to go to the door and look or listen through the keyhole. Listen and learn. But that would never have done, not with the network of ancient spies in the house. So I let myself out by the front door and walked to the leafy avenue to wait for a taxi. I looked at the ground. I was so perplexed. It didn't occur to me that I had yet another huge story on my hands.

I went to the bar in the basement of the Islamabad Grand and sulked at a table eating a dry cheese sandwich and watching a cricket game that was a lot less exciting than the commentators seemed to think. I walked back to the guesthouse and climbed the stairs to my room, hearing the clinking of pool balls on the pink table before I reached the top. That was all I needed. First drums and hissing kettles, now clinking fucking pool balls.

"Eh-up, 'Ad-leh. Fancy a game of pool?"

Oh lord. "Oh, it's you. What a coincidence."

"Aye, it's me. Todd. Yorkshire Todd."

"Todd, of course. What brings you here?"

"Well, it's my nature to be friendly to everyone. So here I am. Fanc-eh a game?"

Did I fancy a game of pool with Todd? Given the choice, I would rather have had my scrotum cut off with a rusting scalpel, folded double three or four times and hammered into shape and glued on to the end of a pool cue. But I didn't say that. Todd was leaning to the side and pulling balls out of the middle pocket.

The angle, catching the light from an ugly elliptical floor lamp, highlighted the cotton wool in his left ear.

My heart sank a little. Then rose a little. I was, after all, a journalist. "Depraved appetites," Marina had said.

"Sure," I said. "What do you play?"

"Stripes and solids. Two shots on a foul. But no backward shots after a foul."

"Sounds good. And if one of us pots the black by mistake?"

"Game over," he said.

"Of course."

"I was wondering. Do you know who I am?"

"I know you found a good Yorkshire 'roob'."

Todd was carefully lining up the triangle, making sure the spot-solid-spot sequence was absolutely right. Bit too fussy, if you'd asked me. I saw cotton wool in his right ear as well.

"I am Colonel Makhdoom's personal aide."

"Oh, I see."

He still wasn't finished with the triangle. "You see, you say. What do you see?"

"I see that security is second to none in Pakistan."

"But it is, Mister 'Ad-leh." He looked up from the triangle. "And that is why I am here. To make sure you are safe. To make sure your visit is secure."

"I feel very secure, thank you, Todd. Thanks to you and the Pakistani security services."

"Who breaks?" he asked.

"Sorry?"

"Shall I break?"

He was talking about the game, not my legs, which was good. "Please, Todd. Chocks away."

He fussed around with the white ball, bending down like a golfer, lining up angles. Just smash the fucker, for fuck's sake.

"I have a role in security that ensures all our overseas visitors are safe," he said, one eye closed as he looked down the table.

"That's great."

"But it behoves our visitors not to take unnecessary risks."

Still he didn't look at me. What did he know? What business

of his was it anyway? Stand your ground, Hadley.

"Risk is my middle name," I said.

Todd looked up. "What did you just say?"

"I mean, this is my business. As a journalist. To find the story. To take acceptable risks." I didn't tell him that I spent five days a week sitting in a comfortable chair editing incredibly boring stories, correcting the possessive of "it" from "it's" to "its". Sometimes I would mix it up and change "its" to "it's".

Todd lined up his shot, his left hand on the table in a fist, not with the fingers splayed. "Oh, I see. As long as we understand one another."

"Of course."

He potted into the pack gently, leaving the white too close to a stripe and a solid up against the left side cushion to give me any chance.

"Sorry, 'Ad-leh. I have the experience, you see. To tuck the white behind coloured balls."

"Terrific break. Well done."

"And while you consider your next move, perhaps I could offer you a word of advice."

I walked around the table, scrutinising my options from every angle. I was fucked. "Of course," I said. I was backed against the cushion with a stripe and a solid a millimetre away. What could I do?

"The colonel's wife is a real lad-eh," he said.

"Yes, I agree. She's magnificent."

"Ah, but she has one habit which is far from lad-eh-like, if you get my drift."

"She has?"

"She gets, how should I say politely, a form of satisfaction from making her husband a green-eyed monster."

"I see."

"That's good. That you see, I mean. He gets jealous. And when he gets jealous, he becomes very passionate, if you follow my line of reasoning."

"I think I do." How could I take a shot with Todd talking non-stop?

"With his wife, I mean. So it's just a word of advice. The colonel's wife can be very affectionate with men. It is a little game. A play."

"I understand completely, Todd." Who the fuck did he think he was talking to? "Thank you so much for the heads-up."

"Aye, just a word of warning, like. Tell me, 'Ad-leh," he said. "Changing the subject if you don't mind. Can you tell me, in a word, which country invented the vacuum suction cleaner?"

Once, twice, three times a lad-eh. Fucked on't table. Fucked in't conversation.

"Funny you should ask that," I said.

"Funn-eh? Why's it funn-eh?"

"No. Sorry. I was being sarcastic. What I meant was: what a strange question." What a *depraved* question.

"Well, do you know, like?"

I stood up straight and thought about it. "Um, at a guess, I would say it would have to be America."

Todd raised his head, picked the chalk off the overhead light and tended to his cue.

"Pakistan," he said.

"I'm sorry?"

"Pakistan. So few people know that."

"Are you sure it's true?"

"You find it unbelievable?"

"No, not at all. I just don't think it's correct." I couldn't concentrate on the game. I tried to pot myself into safety and put the white in the middle pocket.

"Bollocks," I said.

"You think it's bollocks?"

"No, I mean bollocks about that shot. I'll Google the vacuum cleaner."

"That won't give you the full truth."

I wasn't quite sure about the urgency to find out but I pulled out my phone and searched. "Here we go. Vacuum cleaner. Invention. Oh, we're both wrong. Hubert Cecil Booth. England. 1901."

"Well, it would say that."

"You think it's inaccurate?"

"It's heavily biased."

"What do you mean?"

"In favour of the West."

"Why would they lie about who invented the vacuum cleaner?"

"To isolate Pakistan. To make us look weak. I am a senior aide to a Pakistani politician. Look up me and see what you get."

"I don't need to do that," I said. "You have two shots."

"Mister 'Ad-leh."

"No, really. I potted the white. Two shots."

He rested his cue against the glass-panelled door, leant on the table, knuckles against the baize, sighed and shook his head.

"When are you going to see the wood for the trees?" he asked, his head lowered. I could see a bald patch about the size of a sparkly ear ring. He raised his head slowly. His features had changed. Solemn all of a sudden, as he had been in Rick's Cafe. He looked like he had had a stroke.

"The wood?"

"Yes, dear fellow. The wood, like. The big picture."

I looked around the table. "But I potted the white. You get two shots."

He stood erect, turned slowly and picked up his cue. He turned it around so he was holding on to it by the thin end. He raised it above his head and smashed it on the table. Two balls left the surface and headed for the stairs. Bits of wood hit the ceiling. He was looking at me with a slurring, down-turned mouth, a jagged foot of willow in his left hand. One of the guesthouse staff came running up the stairs to see what the commotion was and Todd waved him away.

"I think that may be two shots to me," I said.

Todd picked up the black and threw it through the window. After the smash I heard it bounce once on something hollow. He was leaning on the table again, panting. He mumbled something under his breath.

"Sorry?" I said.

He looked up. "Read my lips," he said. "I insist."

"Insist on what?"

"Don't play games, Mister 'Ad-leh."

"I'm not. I mean, we *were* playing a game. We were playing pool, but you've put paid to that."

"I insist on you being my servant."

Oh lord. Here came the depravity. "Wait a minute. Has it been you calling me at all hours?" As if I didn't know. It made perfect sense. "I don't understand what you just said. I don't know what you want."

"Do not try to delude yourself. It need not take long. But it needs must be done."

"What needs must be done?"

"You know exactly. You must be my servant. Before the Ides of March."

"Before the Ides of March? What are you on about?"

"You see, you see. You are already mocking me. That will never do. I have heard your Roman references. Talking about the Coliseum. I have to insist on you becoming my servant."

Three staff appeared with brooms and dustpans and started to clean up the mess. Not a word of apology from Genghis Khan. And wait. If he had heard me mention the Coliseum with Marina, he had heard the whole conversation. And the colonel. They had heard me stumble at making a pass. They would have heard all she said about men. And about Todd. About him being depraved and violent in the degree of infinity.

"I am a journalist with the Shrubs news agency," I said. "I am not sure what you are asking. I am afraid I have to leave."

"Oh don't be such a fool," Todd said. "Look around you. Look at these men cleaning up the mess around us. The glass everywhere. Doesn't that give you any ideas?"

"I'm afraid not, no."

I was hugely homesick for Hong Kong and anyone who lived within a mile of my New Territories home. The door to my temporary Islamabad home was ten feet away from the pool table and did not offer much in the way of security right there and then. I would head back to the Islamabad Grand. I started downstairs.

"Remember my advice," Todd said.

That was it. I was gone. What a git.

CHAPTER SIX

OUR ISLAMABAD OFFICE is a handsome brick villa with two white-painted arched verandas leading out on to well-tended lawns. Bougainvillea bushes hide the French doors into the high-ceiling rooms of what was once a family house, with extensive kitchens and rooms for the servants. For security reasons, there is no sign saying "Shrubs". We tell visitors to look for the rubbish skip, which is always covered in crows a foot and a half long which flee when anyone approaches, crapping over the grass, the watchman's hut and office cars.

"Mister Hadley, you are back!"

It was my first day in the office since I had arrived. I reached out to shake hands with Shafiq, the affable manager, when an explosion rattled the windows, sending the crapping crows into shrieking panic.

"Stay safe, Marina," I said, surprising myself.

Shafiq and I went to the front door. A plume of smoke was rising from near the law court. Palakorn was ambling up the drive towards us.

"It's nothing," he said. "Some kids playing with pipes."

"Are you sure?"

"They set one off this morning. They're no more than firecrackers." He walked between Shafiq and me into the office. "You can drive off in your fancy car with Marina and leave me here. Believe me, it's nothing."

I introduced myself to the reporters, neither of whom I had

met before. A bully of a bureau chief had sacked all the staff a few years earlier, erasing decades of combined knowledge and integrity with one careless flick of the wrist. I unloaded my things on to a spare desk. Apart from Gary, who wasn't there, there were two text reporters, two photographers and one TV cameraman. My phone went.

"This is Hadley."

"Hadley? Rodney. Opposition running with a bomb exploding near a law court."

"It's nothing, Rodney. Palakorn checked. Some kids playing, that's all."

"Ah, okay."

"Thanks anyway for the heads-up."

"Okay."

The phone rang again.

"Hadley? It's Gary."

"Gary! Good to hear from you. Sorry I couldn't make the party. Are you coming in today?"

"Sorry, I'm out meeting sources. I'm calling because one of those sources said there had been a bomb blast near the office."

"Wow, so quick. Yes, no need to worry. Nothing big. Thanks for the heads-up though."

He hung up. Shafiq came to my desk to introduce someone. My phone rang.

"It's me again." It was Gary.

"Hi."

"An intern is coming in today. I was wondering if..."

"I think she's already here."

"Oh great. Can you do the usual, introduce her to the system et cetera, show her around? I will see her tomorrow. She comes from a very conservative family. Just a heads-up."

"Sure. Leave it with me."

He hung up. A lot of heads were up today.

"Hadley," Shafiq said. "This is Yasmin who is joining us as an intern."

I stood up and shook hands with Yasmin, an earnest woman of about twenty-six with purple lipstick and a loose burgundy-coloured veil partially covering her hair.

"Great to meet you," I said. "I'm afraid Gary isn't coming in today. But please sit down and we can have a little chat."

My phone rang.

"Hadley?"

"Yes."

"It's Fagin, my old China. How's it going?"

"All well, thanks. Kind of busy right now."

"Okay, I'll be brief. We've heard a bomb's gone off."

"It's nothing."

"Okay. That's all I needed to know."

"Thanks for giving me the heads-up."

But imagine if it had been something and you're trying to write the story very quickly and update it constantly as more information came in and every two minutes some bastard rang you to tell you what you already knew. It was infuriating. And you couldn't be rude to these people, because the next time, when it really was important and you didn't already know about it, perhaps they wouldn't bother picking up the phone to call you.

"Sorry, Yasmin, I keep getting these calls about a bomb blast that was nothing. I have to be very polite in how I reply."

"Yes, I saw it. Please, it is of no importance."

That's what I'm trying to fucking tell them, I wanted to say. But I remembered Gary's heads-up. Conservative family. My phone rang again.

"Hadley?"

"This is Susan from London."

"Hi Susan."

"AFP are running a story about an explosion in Islamabad..."

"Thanks Susan. We're on it. Thanks for the head." I hung up. "Zup," I added.

Yasmin was frowning. "I think Susan may be a little confused," she said.

"Indeed. Where were we?"

"You thanked her for the head."

"Yes, I know."

"I am not cognisant of whether it is the same in your country, but the phrase has a connotation..."

"I realise the connotation. It was a mistake."

"She's probably checking back through her diary, ripping through the pages, as we speak."

"Yasmin, drop it, please. Where were we?"

"You were to introduce me to Shrubs. Please explain to me how you send the stories all round the world."

"Ah, now that's interesting."

"Show me, please."

I was distracted, briefly, by two herons bonking on an air-con on the wall of the primary school next door. They were either herons or gannets. They looked very thin and I briefly wondered if they were globally threatened. Good to see them bonking if they were.

"Well, there are different ways," I said. "If it is what we call a bulletin, which is the most important news, like an assassination or coup, you would type just the one line in capitals here. Like this for instance."

I wanted to show her what a funny man I was. I wanted to make her laugh. I didn't want her to think of me as a desk-bound middle-aged fucker who got off watching pigeons getting off on an air-con. Something colourful and edgy. Something about giving head? Too coarse. Something about a politician being blown up outside the Shrubs office? Too close to the bone.

"*Pesky pakistani pranksters' pipe bomb panics pickpockets and promiscuous paramedics,*" I wrote.

Yasmin was frowning again. What the fuck, she was thinking. I could tell. The herons flew off in a cloud of feathers.

"Do all the words have to begin with P?" she asked.

"What? No, of course not."

"How do you know the paramedics were promiscuous?"

"No, you don't understand. They could have been Portuguese for all I know."

"In Islamabad? Really? How do you know? You haven't even looked outside the front door."

"No, Yasmin. You are not getting it. I just wrote those words off the top of my head to show you how we send stories to the world. I was making it up as I went along."

"What happens when I push this button?"

In one smooth, cursive stretch of her right arm, Yasmin, giving off a subtle scent of jasmine, had leant across me and pushed "TRANSMIT", sending my brief, colourful tale about the pickpockets and paramedics to every major newspaper and every major TV and radio station, and plenty more not so major, in the world.

"What the fuck have you done?" I said.

"I don't know," Yasmin said. "Is it something egregious?"

"Egregious? You've just got me fired. *Egregious*?"

I had to think quickly. I copied the bulletin from the TRANSMIT folder and replaced the words with TESTING TESTING and sent it on its way, to tag on to the first bulletin and at least take the sting out of it. The phone went. I hardly dared pick it up.

"What the fuck is this about promiscuous paramedics?" It was Fagin. "Have you entirely lost your mind?"

"I'm so sorry. All my fault. What do we do?"

"What do *we* do? Well, unless we can find some fucking promiscuous paramedics quick fast and hope they've got a story to tell about being panicked – preferably by some pranksters with fucking pipe bombs up their arses... What do you think?"

"I'm going to lose my job."

"You are a complete cunt."

Fagin hung up and both bulletins disappeared from the screen.

Seconds later came the ADVISORY TO EDS (Hong Kong was moving admirably fast) blaming the whole thing on a training error. Brilliant – and true, as it happened.

"I'm going to lose my job," I told Yasmin.

"I am still not very well understanding why all but one of the words began with P."

"No, please, you must stop talking. I am going to go out on the veranda and have a smoke. I shall decide my next move only when I return."

Once out of sight, I took a large swig from my hip flask, lit a cigarette and called Fagin. He would have calmed down by now.

"Am I going to lose my job?" I asked.

"Oh, don't be such a whining Englishman. It's all forgotten already. Things move on. You know how it works. Panic, then total panic, then everything's normal and you wonder what the fuss was about."

"Thank the lord."

"Aye, you can do that."

I went back into the office and apologised to Yasmin for my language and filthy temper.

"It's just that it's never happened to me before," I said.

"But about the pickpockets..."

"No, no, Yasmin. Shut it. I want to move on and tell you a bit about the company, if you are interested."

"I am exceedingly interested."

"Then I shall begin."

I told her the company history I could remember (dropping the bit about complicity in the slave trade before the agency changed its name a couple of times), its commitment to speed and accuracy (there were lamp posts in Islamabad that delivered news faster than we did), its impartiality (Rodney once told me to call the Thai army "heroic" to fend off the threat of a defamation suit). I told her about the staff levels across the world and introduced her to the computer system, showing her how to code and slug a story.

"The slug is what a story is called. We are in Pakistan now, so the first part of the slug will be PAKISTAN, like that." I wrote PAKISTAN in the slug field. "Then, after the country, you will use a word that roughly equates to the story you are writing, which today, if that had been a bigger story, could be BOMB. So we put them together and you get PAKISTAN-BOMB. Today we knew it was a small bomb, but in many cases you won't. You will just hear an explosion, so probably PAKISTAN-BLAST is safer, just in case it turns out to be a passing car or a gas canister. Any questions so far?"

Yasmin was fast asleep. She was snoring evenly and very quietly.

"Hello? Yasmin?"

Shafiq made an urgent entrance. "Hadley, I hate to interrupt but it is important. Look in the drive."

There were two black four-wheel drives. We had visitors from either the government or the military.

"He's here," Shafiq said.

"Who's here?"

"Makhdoom."

"What?"

Shafiq pointed along the corridor to an office used for visitors. There were five men leaning against the wall, looking at me. I wanted to ask Shafiq what I should do. But there really wasn't any choice and to ask the question would have been seen as weak. A giant loss of face.

"What should I do?" I asked. I could see the disappointment on Shafiq's knitted brow. "How did they get in? I never heard a thing. Gary should be here."

"Gary hasn't come in yet."

"Of course he hasn't. Never mind. I know how to handle this. Please give Yasmin some smelling salts if you have any around."

I walked down the corridor, wincing at an abysmal Kenny G

tune on the television next door. If you can't make a sax swing or give it some sex, Kenny, put it back in its case. I nodded my head at the bodyguards and turned into a room where long red velvet curtains let in just a sliver of bright light. With its books, high ceiling fan and heavy, immoveable, hardwood furniture, the room looked just the place for old men in uniform smoking cigars to sign treaties. It was the kind of room that could be recreated in a museum, with waxworks playing the generals and when you touched a button they would lift their arms in a Nazi salute and their eyes would go red.

Makhdoom had his back to me. He had pulled down Mian Langhari's autobiography from the bookshelf, leaving a narrow space between Benazir Bhutto's "Daughter of the East" and cricketer Imran Khan's own autobiography. Gary was a big cricket fan.

"Good afternoon, Colonel. What a pleasure to meet you."

Makhdoom did not look up from the book. He waited a good five seconds before speaking.

"Did you know one of Mian Langhari's greatest pleasures in cricket?" he asked.

"I didn't know he enjoyed cricket. He always looked so glum."

Makhdoom turned. He didn't think that line was funny. Before he spoke I noticed two things: he was out of uniform and wearing braces, both on his trousers and on his teeth. I had never seen them before. He was short and solemn with a tiny, but bushy, moustache and greying hair greased straight back. He wore his trousers high around his stomach like a garden gnome, but without the twinkle in its eye. What makes a man in his mid-forties start wearing braces on his teeth?

"It was beating the English at Lord's." The braces made "Lord's" come out as "Lordth". "On their own turf. Getting one over on the former colonial masters."

"I see."

"With their watery grey eyes, dry hair and blotchy, red faces.

Soapy, soppy Brits. I can say this to you as an American."

Makhdoom was like one of the guys in the bars itching to beat me up.

"No, I am English," I said. "I saw Langhari score a double century at Lord's when I was a kid. But please, don't let me stop you."

"My word. I do apologise."

"No offence taken. I know a few soppy Brits myself. Can I get you some tea?"

"Thank you, but no."

I walked behind the desk, brushing the red curtains, and sat. He knew perfectly well I was a Brit. He knew many things, Marina had said.

"And to what do we owe the pleasure of this visit?" I asked. "Please take a seat."

We looked at one another. He was picking at his teeth with a match. He sat down at the desk.

"When we have visiting journalists in town, it is our responsibility and duty in the military to meet them, to welcome them and to assure them that they are under our protection. Especially during difficult times such as now."

"Difficult times, Colonel?"

"Come, come now, Mister Arnold. There is political instability in this country. There are those who think the situation is so dire that the army should intervene."

"Again."

"Again, yes. To protect the fabric of democracy that is so fragile."

To protect democracy with a coup. Interesting. "Well, thank you. But surely the future of Pakistan is safe, with the likes of your wife running in the election."

"The likes of my wife?"

"Yes."

I wasn't going to curl up and die in front of this prick. The colonel rose from his chair, walked over to the bookshelf and returned Mian Langhari's bodice-ripping best-seller to its place. He paced slowly up and down on the autumn-red Afghan carpet, his eyes lowered, his hands behind his back, one gripping the other by the wrist. He looked like a small invigilator.

"Do you like my wife?" he asked, without looking up.

My testicles rose a fraction and looked around for a place to hide. Here we go.

"I had the pleasure of accompanying her on a campaign stop. I find her very sincere and full of concern for the people," I said. "I am sure she is a valuable asset to Pakistan."

"Thank you, Mister Arnold. I take that as a compliment and a mark of respect for my country. Tell me."

"I must also add that your wife was kind enough to take me to a lovely restaurant." He knew all this, of course. Every word. "She filled me in on the Pakistan situation. It was most rewarding. Sorry, I interrupted."

"Well you have in turn part answered what I was going to ask. We also like to ensure that visiting journalists know something about our country. We do not appreciate prejudice, that sort of thing. Misconceptions."

I wondered if he was aware of my misconceptions about the pickpockets and paramedics. "I understand, Colonel."

"It's just that I have had experience of the Western media. Generally speaking, they know nothing about life and death, about suffering, as many suffer in this country."

"Shrubs is lucky to have excellent Pakistani staff who correct the errors of our ways should we make mistakes. We try to see the big picture. The wood for the trees."

"The wood for the trees. I see." He sat down and crossed his legs. "I have to admit, Mister Arnold, there are many things about the West that confuse me."

"There are many things that confuse me too. All I really want to write about is tea."

"Tea?"

"Eventually, yes. I would like to write about all the different varieties. But right now all that interests me is the Pakistan election. It's quite fascinating. Perhaps you are going to become a first man."

Makhdoom looked at me as though I had said perhaps he was going to become a right dickhead. A cruel and short right charley. His right hand was above his head and he was rubbing his forefinger and thumb together.

"You've come to the wrong country to write about tea, my friend," he said.

"Ah, but I haven't come here to write about tea. I've come here to write about the election."

The colonel was staring. "I was asking my wife just the other day, for example. About the West, I mean. Why is it the Westerners put their parents in prison rather than care for them in old age?"

"Prison?"

"I was wondering why they put their parents in prison and love dogs more than their children. Why is that? Is that a Christian practice?"

"What did your wife say?"

"I'm sorry?

"You said you asked your wife, who is a Christian and has some experience of the West. I wondered what she said."

"She is equally mystified, I believe. Tell me, I am married to a beautiful woman, don't you think?"

"She is very beautiful, yes. And very intelligent."

"Yes. Exactly. I believe half the world probably dreams of my wife." Makhdoom was now examining a nail on his right hand. He was silent. Then he slapped his knees. "I have to leave now, I am afraid." An aide at the door clapped his heels and left the room. The colonel and I rose.

"Are you sure I can't get you some tea?"

"No thank you, Mister Arnold. Let me just say that the foreign press have a window of opportunity to be fair gentlemen in this country."

"I understand."

"Please ensure you seize that window. If anyone were to move away from the window, we security services of Pakistan cannot guarantee your safety. If you seize the window, and we can see you through the window, you shall be safe."

He was over-egging the window motif. "You are coming through loud and clear, Colonel," I said. "As clear as a window, in fact."

"Indeed," Makhdoom said without a flicker of a smile. He looked ready to spit in my face.

He strode down the corridor to the front door which the receptionist was holding open. A sprinkler was making a *toof-toof-toof* noise on the lawn, with the low sun making a rainbow in the spray. He stopped and drew closer.

"Between you and me, Mister Arnold," he whispered. "I have let her little peccadilloes go. But you are English. You are beyond the pale."

"I'm sorry, Colonel?"

"You are an immoral arse. If I ever even suspect another liaison between you and my wife, one of you will be dead by election day."

"What are you saying? You can't say that."

"Enjoy your stay in Pakistan, Mister Arnold."

He marched off to his car. I rushed to my desk and, for the record, wrote down in my notebook what the small bastard had just said. He had threatened me. It was a matter of security and Shrubs took such matters very seriously. If I told Shrubs what he had said, I would have to explain what had prompted him to say it. That's okay. I had done nothing wrong. But if I told Shrubs, I would have to join tele-conferences with all the big bosses and talk bollocks and hear other people talk bollocks. And the end result, not that I had much experience of this sort of thing, would likely be being pulled out of Pakistan for my safety. Bye-bye, Marina, who seemed to be madly in love with someone old enough to be my dad. Shrubs wouldn't run a story about the death threats anyway. It was my word against the colonel's and he was a fucking evil powerful bastard. What was the easiest course of action that wouldn't get me into trouble and that would leave me alone in Islamabad, near Marina, who was crazy about a man who under all the Egyptian scents smelt of urine? Easy. No emails. No tele-conferences. Shut the fuck up.

You don't have to travel far out of Islamabad to find the real Pakistan – dirt poor, feudal, heartless and deteriorating. Life for women, in a country where sexual abuse is euphemistically and hopelessly called Eve-teasing, is particularly brutal. Shrubs had stopped doing stories about honour killings, in which, for example, a teenage girl is stoned to death by her family for smiling at a boy, for looking dreamily out of a window or for singing a few bars of a pop song. The girl has brought dishonour on the family and must be killed. The stories came around too often, each more grisly than the one before it. Being stoned to death for having had sex with someone you love is obscene. Being stoned to death for a wistful smile is just barmy. The sentences are handed down by smug village elders who wallow in corruption, complacency and an evilly skewed interpretation of Islam. Police do nothing to stop them and are all fat fuckers.

That is the backdrop to Marina's visit to her village in the lush farmland of Punjab where she was campaigning, trailed by the foreign press. There was no need to campaign there, because it was safe Pakistan Popular Party territory, but in a country awash with guns where political, sectarian and insurgent violence was rife, it made sense. Any prominent Shi'ite or other minority Muslim was a target in Sunni-majority Pakistan. A prominent Christian was the bull's-eye.

Palakorn, Sultan and I followed her bus on the four-hour drive south, the first stop the burial ground of her forebears. We sat in the back as Sultan shouted stories at us into his rear-view mirror, most involving Western women with large breasts. I was reading the Dawn newspaper website on my phone, a story about a bomb blast at a Protestant church in Peshawar a week earlier that had killed four people. Forensic investigators had found enough bits of the bomb to say that it had been full of ball-bearings and half-inch nails which had been encased in the shell of the motor of a 1945 stand-up Hoover. Bizarre.

Marina sat in the shade of a huge, ancient banyan tree at the burial ground, village supplicants crowding in an arc in front of her. One by one they would approach and bow and scrape and hand over a piece of paper asking for mercy of some sort – help in paying a bill, help to get a son into a good school, to have a word with the village elders to reverse their verdict of death by family on a fourteen-year-old girl who had played hopscotch with a boy. Marina was answering each slowly and compassionately, the older supplicants gripping her hands, effusive in their gratitude, tears in their eyes.

I saw all this but did not understand until Marina told us in a tent where the press were given tea and cakes.

"I help my people whenever I can because they are my people," she said, a cup and saucer in her left hand. "To you Westerners, that may seem backward and patronising, but it is a practice that has gone on for centuries in my country."

"Isn't that the practice of feudalism?" the woman from AFP asked, reasonably enough.

"In the West, you have the luxury of being able to choose from labels," she said. "My people do not have such luxury."

Because they are uneducated and know nothing about democracy. But no one took her up on it. She was too easy a target. And hang on, she had even told me in the car it was time to cut the shackles of feudalism. She used the very word. Why didn't I throw that back in her glistening face? What was the matter with me? I wondered how many people had noticed that her voice was slurring just a tiny bit and her pupils were suspiciously large.

Palakorn came up behind me and grabbed my shoulder. "That's what she said in the car, that it was time to end feudalism. Why didn't you take her up on it?"

"It's all semantics," I said. Palakorn was one hundred percent right. I should have challenged her in front of the TV cameras. It would have gone all over the world.

"Well, it's not for me to tell you your job," Palakorn said, "but it seems you've wasted a bit of ammunition."

"Palakorn," I said, winging it. "Please have some faith in my judgement. If I had challenged her on that, everyone here would have the story. Now only I have the story – that she said she wants to sever the shackles of feudalism, and then promptly dismissed the term as a Western label. It makes her out as a lightweight. A piece of fluff. I can use this at my leisure."

Palakorn thought a while and then patted my shoulder. "Brilliant," he said. And he was off again.

Marina was talking now. "Let us not talk contrarily," she said, handing her teacup to an aide. "I feel we should be bonding. The Western press has been good to me and I want to be good to you. When I do this... " She leant back, raised her arms above her head and rested her long, downward-pointing finger tips on the top of her head in the shape of a heart. "...I will be thinking of you all."

The journalists laughed politely. And her eyes caught mine for an instant, as they must have caught others as well. Still, it made me think – firstly, that she was fucking bonkers, and secondly, that she was somehow thinking only of me.

The next day we arrived at the green, poetic, flawed and ancient city of Lahore where Palakorn and I were standing on a twenty-foot-tall election podium which we had reached by fork-lift truck, standing on the two metal prongs. The ladies and gentlemen of the press were waiting for Marina as the crowds grew below us. I leant on the balustrade and looked across at the charged body of humanity, passion and hope. Good lord. Balloons lifted flags into the sky. Hundreds of huge, green, red and white flags waved over bearded men's heads. I estimated the crowd at 100,000 already. The place was filling up fast and the whole structure, lit up by gantries of spotlights left, right, front and back, insects flapping madly back and forth, was already gently swaying under the pressure of bodies pushing against those in front below. Grown men climbed on to one another's shoulders, they climbed up precarious scaffolding and stanchions, they perched themselves or rooftops and in tall, spindly trees – all so they could wave flags and banners, worshipping someone who would do absolutely nothing to make their lives any better. No one who ran for office had anything other than self-interest at heart. Same the world over. That goes for you too, Marina.

"We'll be lucky if we get out of this alive," Palakorn said. "When's Gary turning up to any of these gigs?"

"Fuck knows," I said. I lit a cigarette. I thought about Makhdoom's threat. Marina was to climb on to the podium by the fork-lift but there was a narrow staircase, declining sharply into heavy security, should she need to get away in a hurry. I crouched down in the corner and took a swig from my hip flask as two helicopters flew low overhead. I must stay away from her. I must not give the colonel any reason to suspect anything. Security men on the podium and on the ground were speaking furiously to one another on their walkie-talkies, looking at the sky. The colonel could get us both here. Kill two birds with one stone. Someone was hanging dangerously out of an aircraft, walkie-talkie at his ear. I looked down and into the glazed eyes of a handful of Marina's supporters dressed in jeans and t-shirts and rubber sandals. Drunk and stoned on nothing, for nothing that happened tonight was going to have any effect. Go out and rob a bank, I thought. One teenage girl, a green veil covering most of her face, was twirling around in circles, carrying a sign that said: "U.S. liberals: Lay Off Malala."

Cheers erupted behind the podium and a few panicky crows took off from leafless trees. The focus of attention was out of vision, but it appeared that Marina had arrived.

"How many people do you reckon now?" I asked Palakorn. He didn't hear me. The podium was getting knocked from each side now. I fell on to a bench for the press. The cheers had risen into a constant wall of noise. I saw Marina now, standing in the back of a pickup truck, all lights, cameras and faces turned towards her.

Her aides and police beat a path before her – her supporters were getting beaten as she approached the fork-lift. Whacked across the ankles, the back, the neck. I saw four men fall lifeless to the ground. Then, safety. Marina and a handful of grey-haired party officials were on the lift and rising. The arc lamps picked her out. Her forehead shone with sweat and the force of nature. She was completely alive. She was on fire. However crappy and corrupt Pakistani politics was, however much she was in love with herself, there was no faulting her bravery.

She reached the top, beaming and waving. Everyone was pushing towards her, and I was being swept along with the flow. I wanted to keep as far clear of her as possible but now I was almost in front of her. She caught my eye and beamed some more. She took off her large sunglasses, pressed forward and leant towards my right ear, away from the crowd. She had to shout against the noise.

"In England, there isn't anywhere near this passion." She leant herself against me in the briefest of hugs.

She drew back and beamed into my eyes again. I beamed back. I had nothing to say. Her pupils were like plates. She leant forwards again.

"In England, you have elections every five years." She pulled back briefly and then went back to my ear. "In Pakistan, my people are not knowing if there will ever be a next one."

"Yes," I said, adding quickly: "Be careful of your husband."

"A million people, Hadley," she shouted. She hadn't heard me.

She turned to the front and raised her arms. The cheers went up, louder than anything I had ever heard. They weren't so much cheers as a collective, primaeval roar. I went to the edge of the podium and looked down. The people looked mad. They were madly in love. They were pleading and screaming "Ma-reen-ah! Ma-reen-ah!"

She put her sunglasses back on and tapped the microphone in front of her, making a knocking noise that echoed back from the squat, straggling street buildings that surrounded the crowd. She spoke about something, probably nothing, in Urdu, prompting wailing and gnashing of teeth. After about fifteen minutes, she slipped into English. It happened so fast, it took me a while to realise and I missed the first bit. And I wasn't catching every word against the roar of the crowd.

"...serfdom a thing of the past. He is a man vital to efforts across the world to put women first, as it should be here in Pakistan. He, and he only, was my inspiration growing up as a young girl in Islamabad. His wisdom, his sense of humour and, of course, his promise that he would never give me up..."

Who was she talking about? Her father? Her fucking husband? Presumably it wasn't Rick Astley.

"...And when he says his heart begins to break when he's considering a proposal to let me go, even today I get indelible goose bumps." Oh lord, no. "I think, oh my lord, you have a master plan to let me go? I don't think so, Mister hot singing Englishman with the quiff."

"Ma-reen-ah! Ma-reen-ah!" the crowded shouted. They hadn't a clue what she was on about. No one had. Only a few faces look puzzled. The girl with the Malala poster was now using it as a bat to hit a ball thrown by a girl the same age.

"Didn't you once say, when I was an innocent teenager, that you were never going to give me up, never going to let me go?"

Marina asked. As stoned as any hippy henge, she raised her arms and broke into song. "It would take a strong, strong man..."

The crowd was wild with delight. She was singing to them! What was she saying? It didn't matter! She was so in love with her people, she cared so much that she was singing to them! But this was surely the end of her political career. Girls in rural villages had been stoned to death for singing pop songs. Pakistan's army-backed press were going to have a field day. Loopy, liberal, promiscuous, Christian, gin-sodden, female, showing her face and singing Rick Astley. What a combination.

No one appeared to give any signal, but her strong, strong security guards were suddenly in motion. One switched off the mike with another booming click and three were leading Marina away. She wasn't struggling. I looked down at the crowd who were still shakin' and rockin' and screamin'. I tried to follow Marina who was being led to the back staircase. A security guard put his hand out to stop me and another asked where I thought I was going.

"I'm with the press," I said.

"You'll fucking pay for this."

The crowd below was pushing hard against the podium as if trying to bring it down. Where was the reason in that? They were her supporters. For fuck's sake. They were rocking it and I heard something metallic and important shriek under the pressure. Marina's aides were beating a path down the narrow staircase as supporters tried to climb up. More bloody madness. They were making slow progress. The fork-lift was climbing and descending as fast as it could, which was very slowly, taking just four passengers each time, holding on to each other for dear life.

"I want to break free," I said to no one.

I felt my phone vibrate in my jacket pocket.

"Hello?"

"Be my servan-ter!"

Oh fuck off, Todd. I looked across the crowd. Could there

really be a million people there? How did she know? It wasn't important. There were thousands directly below us, that much I did know, and the podium was really rocking now. I was trying to imagine the physics of it. The whole thing was covered in cloth and carpet and it was impossible to know how much of this pushing and shoving it could take. Was it made of steel or wood?

A huge, sudden roar. It made me put my hands to my ears. Everyone else had their hands to their ears and we were toppling over in slow motion. Like the carpet was being pulled from under our feet. I thought of the scene in "It's a Wonderful Life" when they're dancing on a retractible stage covering an indoor swimming pool and some punk mischief-maker starts to retract the thing and one by one the dancers fall into the pool. I was sitting down now and couldn't understand why I had fallen over. I was slipping and the carpet was burning my bum and the palms of my hands. I was thinking of the carpet in our living room when I was a kid, black with ugly splodges of white, yellow and blue.

Rick Astley. Any time, any place. Be my servant. This wasn't a dream. This was falling for real. The real McCoy. The slippery slope. Curtains.

CHAPTER SEVEN

I WOKE TO FIND MYSELF strapped to a dentist's chair. Everything around me, the walls, the ceiling, the enamel finish on the basin to my left, was the colour of nicotine. My first thought was not what on earth was I doing here, but rather how retro everything was. Very nineteen-thirties, if not earlier. The dentist's chair looked like a jukebox with limbs, all the chrome bits pocked with rust. Why was I strapped in? Must be for my own safety. But why was I at the dentist's?

My phone rang in my jacket pocket. I could reach it with my right hand but couldn't bring it to my ear. I put it on speaker.

"Hadley?"

"Yes. Who is this please?"

"Thank god you're all right."

"Yes, thank god. Who is this please? I'm at the dentist's."

"It's Rodney, Hadley. Palakorn told us all about it. He said you were in the hospital and that you were fine. Why are you shouting?"

"You are on speaker, Rodney. I don't know where I am. They've put a strap around me. Why would they do that?"

"Probably so you don't fall over."

"Why would I fall over? I am so drowsy and confused."

"Do you remember what happened?"

A man wearing blue surgical scrubs put his head round the door, put his finger to his mouth and disappeared.

"A man just put his head round the door and told me to be

quiet," I said. "It's because I have you on speaker. So I am talking a bit more quietly now."

"Hello, Hadley, are you there?"

"Hello, Rodney. Yes, I am here. But I am unable to put the phone to my ear. Because of the straps. What time is it?"

"It must be ten in the morning your time. Hadley, do you remember what happened?"

"It's coming back to me. An explosion. The thing collapsed. The stage. Isn't it good, Pakistan wood?"

"Hadley, hang in there. You are going to be fine."

"Yes, I'm fine thank you. Why am I at the dentist's? I think that was the hygienist who put his head round the door."

"Okay, well good luck with that. I will talk to you later in the day."

"Don't go, Rodney. I have to tell you things. But I mustn't shout."

Colonel Makhdoom appeared at the doorway, dressed head to toe in white, a chrome light on his forehead, a cigarette between his lips and a mallet in his right hand.

"Perhaps we could talk later," Baxter said.

"Baby please don't go."

"Not a good line. Take care, Hadley."

"But..."

The colonel took the phone from my hand and hung up. It promptly rang again. I stared at him. Reluctantly he gave it back.

"Hadley?"

"Yes."

"This is Gary."

"Oh Gary." I was choking up a bit. "I'm so glad to hear from you."

"Why are you shouting? Look, I don't have much time. Can I give you a couple of paragraphs over the phone?"

"What's that Gary? Can you give me what? Can you help me, is that what you are asking? I need some help."

"For fuck's sake, what's the matter with you? Can I give you a couple of graphs. I'm at the central bank."

"A couple of graphs on what, Gary? I'm so confused."

"On the rupee. The central bank's issued a statement on the third tranche of the IMF loan. They're livid. They're thinking of buying up billions worth of government bonds. It's quantitative easing, Pakistan style."

"Is it, Gary?"

"What? Are you ready?"

"Not really, Gary. I'm at the dentist's."

"What?"

"And the dentist is holding a mallet."

"What the fuck are you on about?"

"I think you may have missed quite a big story, Gary. There was an explosion, you see."

"An explosion?"

"Yes. And I don't know what quantitative easing means. In the big picture, I don't think your story is very important. I am with Colonel Makhdoom, who is very important. I am a bit woozy, but he is holding a mallet..."

The colonel took the phone and turned it off. He clicked the side button to red, turning it to mute, and placed the phone and the mallet on the counter. He took the cigarette out of his mouth, lifted his foot on to a metal pedal and pumped. I was rising to the vertical.

"Before I look inside your mouth," Makhdoom said. "have you had any recent problems with your teeth? I did give you ample warning."

The seriousness of the situation was dawning on me through whatever had put me to sleep. The man was a qualified dentist, I knew. But why was he smoking? Dentists don't smoke. He put his cigarette in an ashtray propped up between the drill bits.

"People generally think: 'I am not going to tell you if I have any problem with my teeth. It's up to you, the dentist, to find if there is a problem. Why would I make it easy for you to hurt me?' Is that how you feel, Mister Arnold? I did warn you."

"Nurse," I said.

"Now, now, Mister Arnold, there is no nurse. You know that. I don't need a nurse for what I am going to do inside your louche mouth."

"You don't have the certificates." What was I saying? I had been drugged. More bits and pieces were coming back to me. Marina. Where was Marina? I was at the campaign rally. There was an explosion and I fell and kept falling.

"What certificates might they be? Marriage certificates? I have a marriage certificate. It says I am married to my wife. To the woman you embraced. In front of the whole country."

"What have you done to her?"

"I did warn you. But one thing at a time, Mister Hadley Arnold." He picked up the cigarette.

"What are you doing to me? Why am I strapped down?"

He put the cigarette in the corner of his mouth, squinting against the smoke, and held up a pair of tarnished forceps that looked like sugar tongs.

"Please," I said. "I fell over. But there is nothing wrong with my teeth."

"You fell and you took quite a knock."

There was quite a knock at the door and another man put his head round and slowly entered.

"Hello, Hadley. Can I come in?"

The man didn't wait for me to answer. Obviously English, wearing a blue blazer and beige slacks, he approached the foot of the bed. I was confused but never more pleased to see a fellow countryman, even if he looked like an inbred royal berk. He had no chin and his front teeth stuck out over his lower lip. His nose was shot purple with broken blood vessels.

"I say, welcome back to the land of the living," he said and I could smell the whisky straight off. "Ah Colonel, I did not see you there. How is our patient? Has he been smoking, the naughty boy? Should we expel him from the sanatorium?"

What the fuck was he on about? The colonel stepped forward and shook hands with him, holding the mallet in his left hand behind his back.

"Your Excellency," he said. "It is an honour as always."

"Well I wish it were under happier circumstances, Colonel, but delighted your wife, our dear Marina, is safe."

"Yes, delighted," Makhdoom said. "As always. My eternal thanks."

The Englishman turned to me.

"I am so sorry, Hadley, my fine fellow, you must excuse my tardiness in introducing myself when you must be so dazed and confused ."

"I'm afraid I don't know where I am. I haven't been smoking. The dentist is a heavy smoker."

"Well, let me introduce myself first, if you don't mind, eh? I am David Creasel, the British high commissioner. We have had a bit of a security scare, but you are safe now."

"How is Marina?"

Creasel put his left thumb in his right nostril and made an oafish face and blew out sharply of the left nostril. It was like taking snuff in reverse. "Perhaps you would like to explain, Colonel?"

"My wife is very safe, thank you for asking, Mister Arnold," Makhdoom said. "She is a little shaken, but she is fine."

"Why are you holding a mallet in your left hand?" I asked. "Why am I here?"

"Now, now there, Hadley," Creasel said. "You are very confused. The colonel is a jolly famous dentist. He wants to see if there is any permanent damage."

"He said I had a louche mouth."

"I should fetch the doctor," the colonel said. He left the room.

"I am not making this up," I said. "I need protection from him.

I admit I am a little confused. Why is he walking around with that mallet? Is he a carpenter?"

"You were very lucky," Creasel said, sitting in a tatty leather armchair under a revolving fan and crossing his legs. He gave his right nostril another feel. "The stage fell in such a way that most of you chaps on top slid most of the way before coming to an abrupt halt."

"Slid?"

"You were on the podium with Marina Makhdoom. Someone threw an explosive device, I am afraid. The stage fell and you tumbled off it with a few bumps and burns and bruises. Your bottom is worse for wear, I should suspect. A bit rosy, perhaps?"

"Rosy? My bottom is rosy? What are you talking about? I don't feel any pain. Certainly there is nothing wrong with my teeth. I don't need to see a dentist. Was anyone killed?"

"I am afraid there were casualties, yes. At least a dozen on the ground and two security men on the podium. None of Marina Makhdoom's people was hurt, nor any journalists."

"Sir."

"You can call me David."

"The colonel did it."

"Now, now, there. You have no such evidence."

"I know it. Mark my words. And Marina was talking and then ... she was talking nonsense. I know I have been drugged. I feel... squiffy."

"Well, she appears to have had a turn of some sort. She is seeking rest and attention in Hong Kong."

"But the colonel, sir. Sir David. He's not what he seems."

"He has a reputation for being a bit of a card, it's true."

"No, he's not a card. The other day he threatened to kill one of us by election day."

"One of us?"

"Not you. He meant me or Marina. She must be a huge embarrassment, of course. Her political career in tatters. But don't think of him as a card. He is dangerous. He thinks..."

"Yes? What does he think?"

"He thinks there is something going on between me and Marina."

"Oh good gracious. Does he, indeed?"

"I know it sounds ridiculous, but yes. He thinks I've been giving her one."

"My dear chap, I know you are a bit dizzy, but let's not resort to the talk of the gutter, eh?"

"He's strapped me in. Look. Why would he strap me in? He gets off on the jealousy, you see."

"Gets off on the jealousy? I would hazard a guess that he has strapped you in for your own comfort. May I suggest you get some well-earned rest?"

"He hates the English."

"Now, now, Hadley."

"I have been very respectful to his wife. But he said I was beyond the pale. He probably thinks you're a toffee-nosed git."

The high commissioner shifted in his chair and folded his legs. "I have known the colonel, and his charming wife, for many years," he said. "I believe our friendship is genuine and deep-rooted. It is certainly supported by evidence."

"He thinks I deep-rooted her."

"Oh now, really," Creasel said, rising from the chair. "I am going to get the doctor. Ah, emergency over. Here come the dentist and the doctor. How splendid. Where's the colonel's handsome aide?"

Handsome aide? Did he mean loopy Todd? Good lord. And what on earth was splendid about any of them?

"So, Hadley. Just the ticket," Creasel said. "I must take my leave."

"No, don't go."

"Ha ha, indeed. Give this man some more drugs. And here's wishing you a quick recovery and bon voyage."

"I don't want to stay here."

"Be a brave old chap, eh?"

He shook my hand, said "gentlemen" to the young, balding doctor and the colonel, and was gone.

"Now Mister Arnold," the doctor said. "We're going to have you out of here in no time."

"And here's a friendly face to expedite your recovery," the colonel said. The doctor laughed and the colonel showed me his braces. Without taking his eyes of me, he shouted: "Enter!"

A man slid round the door jamb into the room, a playful smile on his face.

"Eh-up 'Ad-leh."

Oh lord.

"Do you wish to attend to some dental work, now, Colonel?" the doctor asked. "Or can we let him rest?"

"I'll just take a little look."

"All right, then." And then to me. "I will be leaving now. I'll be back to see you before, you know..."

No, I didn't know. "Doctor, please don't leave."

"You're in good hands, Hadley."

The doctor left the room. And the colonel walked towards me. He gave the mallet to Todd.

"I hope you will let me inspect for damage, Mister Arnold," the colonel said as he put on rubber gloves. "I am seriously most interested. Please open wide."

I did as I was told, small tears emerging in the corners of my eyes. The colonel prodded around and pushed here and there. Then he inserted his thumb and pushed a bit harder on my top teeth.

"There's nothing wrong," I said when he had removed his hand.

"I would beg to differ, Mister Arnold. You have a nastily chipped canine."

"Where?"

"Open wide."

I did as I was told. The colonel put a prod against one of my back teeth. I kept having to swallow, each time making a short, dry gagging sound. I saw Todd hand something to the colonel who in one swift move tapped the mallet on the prod.

"Right there," he said.

"What are you doing?" I asked, pulling my head away. "You've just broken my tooth!" I hadn't felt any pain but there were bits of shrapnel in my mouth. "Why did you hit my tooth with a mallet?"

"I am exorcising the excoriated enamel."

"Oh no you're not."

"Oh yes I am."

"I don't know what you are saying. But you just broke one of my teeth."

And then *thwump*, Todd to the left of me and the colonel to the right slapped metal arm brackets over my wrists. My feet were pulled back as if by rope and I was immobile.

"You must trust us," the colonel said. "Todd is my very efficient security aide. You must obey his commandments."

"Aye, 'Ad-leh. Not so much commandments as requests, like."

"You have damaged one tooth and I am going to make it right for you," the colonel said. "I need to entrain a lower portion of the tortial bell..."

"What?"

"For which I suggest you accept a ready offer of an anaesthetic."

"Anaesthetic? Why?"

"For the entrainment."

"Look, I don't need any entrainment. I don't even think there is such a word. Except in a Van Morrison song. You must let me go. I am a foreign correspondent and you cannot get away with this behaviour."

"You are foreign matter who thinks he can make a cuckold of me."

"I have not made a cuckold of you. You must let me go."

"I shall let you go, eventually. But do not consider the option of writing any schoolboy fantasy story about me, or my aides, or, indeed, my wife with her loose Christian morals. Open your mouth."

Again, I did as I was told. I couldn't bear the alternatives. I stared wildly, running my fingers under the cold, metal lips of the armrests. Makhdoom reached up and adjusted the light on his head. He was making slight gasps. His face was set in an ugly grimace. He dropped his prod in the metal tray and took a syringe from Todd, held it up to the light and tapped it. It was a big, glass affair, a type I remembered from my childhood, with a fat needle that was usually more painful than the procedure to follow. Though in this case, I was willing to hedge my bets. Had he knocked all the bubbles out? Or was he going to really hurt me and give me an embolism and the bends to boot? The colonel was looming now. I was trying to pull away. I tried to bang my head from side to side, but Todd held me back in a vice. In he came. I could smell the coconut oil on his hair, tobacco on his moustache.

"Now this may hurt a little," the colonel said.

There was, surprisingly, just a gentle sting. He knew what he was doing! How extraordinary. I wanted to thank him, but could not speak. Such is the gratitude of the victim, overcome by the smallest act of kindness from the torturer.

"Let's give it a couple of minutes to take effect," he said.

But why all this adherence to protocol when all he wanted to do was hurt me? He wasn't worried about my teeth, that was for sure. But he was back in my mouth, poking around. I could feel the steel probe in his hand sticking to the tooth in places as I watched an orderly push yet another stretcher loaded with lead bars along the corridor outside.

"There's a bit of entrainment here," the colonel said, turning to swap his probe with another, thinner, stick-insect like gimlet.

"I am going to stick this instrument into the entrainment and push a little. As far as it will go, in fact."

"Ooorph," I said.

"I want to make sure the anaesthetic has taken effect. Here we go. It may hurt a little. One, two, three..."

In the tiniest fraction of a second, I had ripped both armrests off their mountings and tears had launched themselves out of my eyes on to my shirt. My first thought was of an electric chair, and something going disastrously wrong with the voltage, or wattage or ampage or something, and everyone above me looking at each other as if to say *what do we do now?*

"I do apologise," Makhdoom said. He had picked up the anaesthetic phial. "Use before 1947, it says. Independence. Partition. How did I not see this?"

He disappeared behind me. My mind was racing. It was running the whole gamut of deliberately administered pain through the centuries. I thought of sixteenth century Spanish Catholics in the pretty city of Ronda just an hour from the Costa del Sol. I thought of Ben Hur on his slave boat. I thought of trying to make head or tail of "Twelfth Night". Funnily enough, I didn't think of Dustin Hoffman and Laurence Olivier in "Marathon Man" and dentist Olivier asking: "Is it safe?"

The colonel came back into vision with another syringe but did not say anything. He injected the back right-hand side of my mouth, again with the gentle sting. He stepped back and looked at me disgustedly.

"The operation begins now," he said.

Then Todd spoke to the colonel, making some kind of a plea. The colonel spoke fast in Urdu to Todd in response. Todd pleaded again and the colonel raised his voice in a long reply and slapped Todd on each cheek. Makhdoom took off his white jacket and the light on his head, leant towards me and undid all the straps and contraptions.

"He's all yours," he said to Todd. And then to me: "I am

assured that my aide has some unfinished business with you of which I am honour-bound to let him partake." What the fuck? "I ought to tell you, Mister Arnold, a bit about Todd's background. As a child, he was forced to be a servant to a Pashtun warlord in the northern Afghan town of Mazar-i-Sharif who went by the name of Felix the Cat." Todd was looking bashful, as well he might, staring at the ground and playing with the linoleum with his right foot. "Then he was sent packing to one of your indescribably corrupt public schools at which he was forced to serve tea to prefects in their beds while wearing nothing but a woolly hat."

"I don't want to hear this shit," I said. "Let me out of here."

"Ah, but you must let me finish. Things took a turn for the better. After school he joined a firm of lawyers..."

"Accountants," Todd said, still looking at the floor.

"My apologies. Accountants, again in England, at which they forced him to clean the lavatories wearing nothing but..."

"Ballet shoes."

"Ballet shoes."

"I don't hold any grudges, 'Ad-leh," Todd said. "I just like to see the tables turned for once, like. For people to be my servant, but in a most respectful manner."

Makhdoom left without so much as a goodbye, closing the door gently behind him. He was leaving me to Todd? What on earth did he want to do to me? The right side of my head was numb. The right side of my body was numb. Todd's head came into vision, a big smile on his face.

"Eh-up," he said.

I waved my left arm in anger, knocking a plastic glass from the basin, and kicked my left leg weakly. What had the colonel done to me? I was at this nutcase's mercy. Again I kicked and waved limbs on the left, but it was mere floundering.

"I hate to see you in distress," Todd said. "But at least we are here together." He leant back against the counter, raised his head, looked at the ceiling and sighed. He pulled out a cigarette and lit it. "But we still haven't reached any sort of common ground, have we? You refuse to meet me halfway. You put me through the mill again and again."

Trouble down't mill. If only he could drown down't mill pond. He stepped outside the door and within a minute was back carrying a basket and pulling some contraption with squeaky wheels into the room, the cigarette in his mouth. It was an old stand-up Hoover. It had a black, perpendicular, deflated bag above a tiny, steel sucking device shaped like the head of a fly with one, large, beige, bulbous eye. So it seemed to me at the time, anyway. It had a curved, corrugated, black Bakelite handle and was probably the most hi-tech piece of machinery in the building.

"Now I know you're drugged up something proper," Todd said. "The colonel warned me. He said it would take a few minutes to wear off and you would be fit as a fiddle. My intervention has saved you some real pain at the hands of the colonel, I reckon."

I looked at Todd and I looked at the Hoover. Todd was leaning on it now, playing with the cord.

"I think by now you have a sneaking suspicion of what's going through my mind," he said. "How you can say 'thank you' to Yorkshire Todd."

I flapped my left arm once. I just wanted this man to go away somewhere and explode. Just like, I only now remembered, that Hoover had exploded in the Peshawar church.

"When you're ready, and there's no hoor-eh," he said, pushing the Hoover closer to me. "But I'd be ever so grateful if you could run this around for me. There's nothing so very troubling about that, is there? The room is particularly dust-eh and I am a little done in."

I looked at Todd and back at the Hoover. I could feel a heavy tingling on the right side of my body. The anaesthetic was wearing off. Todd hadn't finished.

"I am just going to pop out and freshen up and get into the appropriate attire. Then I am going to slip into that bed over there while you ... well, while you do for me. With the Hoover."

Todd left the room. I could feel my right leg now. I could move it. I tapped the right side of my head and it gave a sensory version of the ringing of a deep bell. I was getting back together. I rose from the supine to sit in the dentist's chair. I looked back at the bed that Yorkshire Todd had his heart on climbing into as soon as he came back. Good lord, what was the matter with him? I stood up and walked gingerly over to the Hoover and leant on it for support. There was a picture on the back of the black bag, a Christmas ad, no less. A white American woman, wearing a tight-fitting pink dressing gown, was kneeling by the side of the same model Hoover with a big, red Christmas bow tied to the handle. She was obviously overjoyed at her husband's generosity. "Give her a Hoover and you give her the Best," it read. How could that be? What were they talking about?

"Oh bless!"

Todd had returned. He was wearing striped pyjamas and carrying a purple Barney dinosaur under his arm. He ran and jumped on to the bed and was under the covers within a few seconds.

"You know what this means to me, don't you 'Ad-leh?"

"I don't understand anything," I said.

"Plug it in please."

"Sorry?"

"Plug the fucker in. In the wall."

Was I strong enough to lift this thing and clock the git over the head? Hang on, maybe the colonel had left his mallet.

"'Ad-leh, you must plug the cord in over there by the door. Then you can run it around. And you will see a little bag clipped to the handle. Yes, that one. It contains an extension and some accessories. There is one that is very good for getting down the sides of chairs and under antimacassars and such. But never mind those for now."

"Okay," I said. "I'll plug it in now."

"If you will, please."

"I won't worry about the accessories for the moment."

"Correct."

Todd snuggled down as if about to be read a bedtime story, pulling the sheet up to his chin. There was one thing clear in my head: nothing would make me return to that bed tonight, even if it had been stripped of its linen and boiled in gin. One way or other, I was out of there. My clothes were in the cupboard with my shoes. At some point I had to gather them and make a run for it.

I plugged the Hoover in and walked back to the machine and stepped on the metal switch. The thing roared slowly to life, the black bag swelling and dust rising to my nose without my even having moved the bloody thing. Todd clapped his hands twice, his eyes on the head of the fly, a really stupid, childish grin on his face.

I Hoovered around the hardwood edges first, quite surprised at how much dust had collected in a narrow stretch between the wall and the floor. The Hoover was doing a great job getting to those hard-to-reach places. The suction was magnificent.

"You bastard," Todd said above the din. I looked at him briefly. He still had his eye on the fly's head.

I got the machine on to the carpet and it was drawing the pile deep into its heart, giving it a right old battering and letting it go as good as new!

"This reall-eh is the Best," Todd shouted over the noise of the engine. "Look at the action!"

There was no security on the door. I had to take my chances. I just needed a couple of minutes' head start. I already had my passport, a standard routine for correspondents in dodgy territory. And it didn't get much dodgier than this. I could go straight to Islamabad airport and get on the next plane to anywhere. Or should I take a taxi back down to Lahore and take a plane from there? By that time, though, they could have sealed off all the airports. But would they really go to such lengths? For what reason? This was personal between me and the colonel, and Todd was just barmy. There were no issues of national security surely. My head was in a spin. I couldn't decide.

"'Ad-leh?"

"Yes Todd." The berk was holding his Barney against his chest.

"When you've done with the Hoovering, I want you throw a duster around."

"Okay."

"I haven't quite finished. After that, there is a sink load of washing up that needs to be done."

"A-hah."

"A-hah? Why do you say that?"

"Where is the sink?"

"It is round the corner in your private kitchenette. Turn right and it's off the main corridor on the right. I want to hear the clatter of plates and saucepans, do you hear?"

"Of course."

"That's more like it. You'll find all you need in my basket. Now carr-eh on."

I started Hoovering again – and Todd started singing.

"*Now hands that do dishes can be soft as your face, with mild, green Fairy Liquid.*"

I was Hoovering under the bed now, amazed at how low the handle would go, almost horizontal, without the cleaning heads lifting off the carpet. The engineering was far ahead of its time. After that, I had pretty much done. It was time to do a bit of dusting. I stepped on the metal button and the Hoover moaned down an octave to silence. I would ride my luck. I was wearing a hospital shalwar kameez, a long, white cotton shirt over baggy, cotton trousers. I would forget my clothes. I would just grab my shoes and go. First a bit of dusting. I made a fuss of the broken

Venetian blinds, so Todd could hear me at work. The blinds covered darkened windows. There was no natural light coming into the room. Todd wasn't moving at all, just staring at the floor. Then I tried some silent dusting, to see how long he would go before registering. I went back to the blinds. I looked over. His eyes were shut.

It was now or never. I opened the cupboard as gently as I could and took my shoes. I looked at my clothes and changed my mind. I lifted them gently down from the hangers, one of which banged against the wood. I stopped and looked towards the bed. No sign of arousal, thank the lord.

I tip-toed out the door, looked right towards the "kitchenette" and left towards the staircase and freedom.

"Dusting duties over, are they, 'Ad-leh?"

I dropped my pile of clothes out of sight in the corridor and turned.

"Pretty much, Todd," I said. "I thought I'd get on with the pots and pans."

"Aye, and make sure you get 'em gleaming."

"I'm on it."

Who had been using pots and pans in my kitchenette anyway? The food I had had, a really nice chicken curry with dal, was brought in by a uniformed soldier from a trolley. I found the place and there was one saucepan that looked like it had been used to make some milky tea. I looked around and opened a couple of drawers. I opened a cupboard and found Todd's clothes. I went through the pockets of his jacket. Cigarettes, tickets of some sort, a newspaper cutting in Urdu about Marina (her picture was at the top), a box of swimming earplugs and a big ball of cotton wool.

I returned to my room (my room? Hah!) with a large aluminium tea tray under my arm and went to Todd's bedside. He had his head under the sheet

"Excuse me, Todd."

He came to the surface. "Yes, what is it?"

"I can't find the Fairy Liquid."

"The Fairy Liquid?"

"Yes. For the pots and the pans. And this tray."

"You want to wash the tray?"

I brought it out from under my arm and inspected it. It was round, large, sonorous and just the job.

"I don't think anyone has cleaned it in months," I said. It was now or never. There was nothing in Todd's ears. "I'm a bit of a perfectionist about these things."

At that second, the electricity failed. The room was in darkness. It would be at least ten seconds before the generator kicked in, maybe less in a hospital (though I wasn't prepared to put money on it). I raised the tray above my head. I had to make a very fast decision – whether to bring the tray down on Todd's head, or...

I brought it down smack on the empty top of the nicotine-coloured metal chest of drawers next to the bed with a loud crack. The lights came on. I looked at Todd. His mouth was open as if I had indeed brought it down on his head. His eyes were closed and he had fallen back on the pillow. It seemed to have worked. But for how long? The lights went out again, presenting me with too good an opportunity to miss. I hit Todd's head with the tray with a sonic boom. Perhaps that would wake him up? I started hitting him with the edge of the tray in the neck area. I wasn't sure what I was trying to do. Did I want him dead? A soldier came skidding to a halt at the door.

"What was that altercation noise, please?"

"I'm sorry," I said. "I dropped the tray. Didn't mean to alarm anyone. The colonel's aide appears to have nodded off."

"This is a hospital," he said unnecessarily. "He is reposing in your bed."

"Yes."

"Having a sleep, I am supposing."

I looked down at Todd, where he was reposing as the soldier

was supposing.

"I think that's correct," I said.

"He looks very thoughtful when reposing. As opposing to when he is wakeful and… careless."

"That's a very good assessment," I said. "He is a careless man."

The soldier, each hand holding the door jamb, looked around the room briefly and then up at the ceiling. "We have to be on the alert for improvised explosive devices," he said.

"Of course. Thanks for getting here so quickly."

"It is my duty, sir."

"Funnily enough," I went on, "talking about duty, the doctor suggested I get some fresh air and perhaps walk in the streets a while. Would you please show me the way?"

I FOUND A SUZUKI MEHRAN and asked the driver to take me to a Mongolian restaurant and guesthouse I knew where the Ethiopian owner made wonderful kimchi and had a supply of Black Label. I rang Baxter in Hong Kong to tell him where I was and that I was lying low with yet another stomach bug. No one else knew. I would pick up my stuff from the Chateau Hill later.

"But Hadley, we haven't had any stories out of you! When do you plan to file?"

"I have a great story. Don't you worry about that."

"Well, when will we see it?"

"Not long now, I reckon."

What story did I want to give him? What story could I safely write anyway? Right then, I just wanted to escape.

"But I know nothing about it," Baxter said.

"Rodney, believe me when I say the walls have ears. Allow me a little leeway. Please. I have to lie low."

"Lie low?"

"For a while."

The security people had tracked me down to my village home in rural Hong Kong easily enough. How long before they found me in their own backyard? I had to get out in the open and sit quietly somewhere and think things through.

I spent the afternoon watching cricket under the hills. Crows flew low over the wicket and settled on a rusting mower that had lots of dry chains and appeared at least a hundred years old. They took off, back the way they had come, and landed on the dilapidated scoreboard. I sat on a bench and relaxed. A few people were jogging round the pitch, the women not daring to show an inch of ankle. Even the few men wearing shorts were wearing very long shorts.

"You are walking in a wrong directing (sic)," a white sign next to the jogging track said. "Please walk anti-clockwise and cooperate with other walkers."

A man was sitting high on a large, green roller dating back to the late nineteenth century, rolling a piece of grass which wasn't part of the pitch. Four goats were grazing beside the pavilion. The players were pumped up and screaming encouragement at each other. "Nice ball, nice ball, nice ball, nice ball, nice ball!" a young man on the near boundary was shouting in a crescendo, again and again, ending with a high-pitched: "Good bowling!"

"Well fielded," another fielder said plummily to his mate at deep silly point. I briefly thought of Mian Langhari taking pleasure in beating the English at "Lordth" and realised I was biting my nails. What was going on? Why was I in Pakistan? What did these people, and I meant Marina, her sadistic husband and his barmy Yorkshire aide, want from me? The stress was beginning to take its toll. I was staring at a cloud formation over the hills that looked like a woman in a burqa running away from a puppy.

My next thought was that the hills were tumbling. No, they weren't. I could see them, dark in the lowering sun. So Islamabad had been struck by an earthquake. No it hadn't. The pavilion to my right was stable and still. The white-flannelled cricketers were still playing cricket and the goats weren't looking at each other and saying "what the fuck?". I was on my back on the ground and nothing was making sense. All of these frantic mind games took place in a millisecond before I realised what was going on. The ancient roller had flattened the left-hand, iron upright of the slatted bench with me its next target and there was no one driving the bloody thing. The pitted rolling mechanism was less than a foot from my sprawled legs and gaining. I dragged myself backwards, my elbows taking the grasshopper position, and I felt the iron brush my extended right toe. I dragged myself back some more and rolled to the side and watched the machine flatten what was left of the bench into the grass. A couple of the cricketers ran over to see if I was okay as the rolling machine continued its path towards the goats. One man jumped up and pulled a few levers and pushed a few buttons until the thing stopped.

"Are you okay?" he shouted.

"I'm fine. What happened?"

"Someone was driving it over there," one cricketer said, pointing to the far boundary. "And suddenly it was over here. *Sans* driver."

That was about the size of it. I didn't know quite what to say.

"Did you see where the chappie went?" another cricketer asked.

But no one had. "The irresponsible fellow had obviously forgotten to turn off the keys," one said. Right.

I said thank you, bade my farewells and headed for the Margalla Road. So much for staying out in the open. The plan now was to get a taxi back to the new guesthouse, where no one knew I was, and bolt myself in my room. My legs were a little shaky. A car, another Suzuki Mehran, pulled alongside. Colonel Makhdoom rolled down the window with stiff turns of the handle.

"Get in, Mister Arnold."

"Hello Colonel. It's fine, thank you. I want to walk."

"I won't ask again."

"I need the exercise. You look very big in that car."

"So be it."

I started off down the street and looked back to see if I could cross. What I saw was a thug with a jet black wig swept diagonally across his forehead get out of the back of the car. I ran across the road, not really looking to see if it was safe. Yet another Suzuki Mehran passed at speed, honking its horn. Actually it wasn't really going at speed and the honking was more like a gargle, but I was still lucky not to have been run over. The colonel's thug waited for the car to pass before crossing the road at his leisure. The colonel's driver sped up the road and did a u-turn a hundred yards ahead and parked a dozen steps in front of me. The thug had me in a bear hug and marched me to the car and into the tiny back seat. It was an awful squash.

The car headed into the hills above the cricket pitch, manoeuvring a series of hairpin bends with all the grace of a cement mixer. Everything was passing us on blind corners, one an open-top truck with about ten colourfully dressed men hanging off the back. Three women on a motor scooter overtook at speed, looking across at us, and one back at us, with disappointment etched into their brows.

"Where are you taking me?" I asked.

From this height, the city was flat with one or two noticeable landmarks – the Faisal Mosque below us and the Rawal Lake to the left and a sprinkling of high-rises, among them the world's ugliest building, the Saudi Pak Tower. We passed an outside restaurant called the Monal, with kebab barbeque smoke partially blocking the view of the city, and were then flanked by fir trees on the right and a sharp drop to earth-roofed huts and tiny, green wheat fields on our left. Lines of washing were stretched over swept, dry mud. The car pulled off the road, the earth-roofed huts below, and parked between small boulders that had fallen through the fir trees on the steep bank on the other side of the road.

"You will get out here, Mister Arnold," the colonel said.

He opened his door and climbed down, raising his arms and stretching. The thug next to me gave me a push towards the door. I did as I was told.

"You will follow me, please."

The driver stayed in the car. The colonel walked first, followed by me with the bewigged thug taking up the rear. The colonel stopped and kicked something on the ground. He was scratching at something with his foot, occasionally looking up and down the road to make sure no one was coming. He said something in Urdu.

The something he was scratching at was a concrete manhole cover about eighteen inches in diameter. I was suddenly so homesick. I breathed in deeply to disguise a giant blub. The thug walked forward with a crowbar in his hand. This had all been planned. He worked it around the edge of the cover then prised the thing away. It was about five inches thick and obviously heavy. I looked into the hole, not quite believing that anyone could perpetrate such horrible violence on me. From a pool of water at the bottom to the top was at least three feet. It was impossible to tell how deep the water was.

"Get in, please," the colonel said.

How could I break this spell? How could I get them to realise that this was a cruel thing to do? To me, of all people. To this affable Englishman travelling with them in these majestic hills.

"Stroll on, Colonel." I tried to make light of it, to make him see that he had to be joking. "I mean, do me a favour. I'm not going in there."

The thug picked me up and dropped me into the hole like a stone. I had no idea if there was an inch of water at the bottom or two feet. Or twenty feet for that matter. So I had no idea when to brace for contact, a sure recipe for a broken ankle at the least. I stuck my feet against the circular wall to slow my descent, which threw my right shoulder hard against the wall, and I struck bottom within a second without any searing pain. I was standing in about a foot of water, my head peeping over the top of the manhole at road level, looking up at the face of Colonel Makhdoom silhouetted against the now darkening sky.

"I can pick you up in the street with impunity, Mister Arnold. I can drop you in a hole. Do not be under the misapprehension that I cannot do more."

I fought my way through the negatives to arrive at what he meant: Next time he would kill me.

"I'm with the press," I said. It didn't come out as confidently as I had hoped. I choked on "press".

Makhdoom looked at the sky. He looked down at me and in one swift move, he undid his fly and pulled out his dick.

"I'm sorry," he said. "I didn't realise you were a gentleman of the press." He was waving his prick in circles now but nothing was happening. "Next time I shall have much more respect. Onward Christian bloody soldiers."

I tried to duck out of the way, but the narrow hole only allowed me to duck my head. And then... nothing came. I looked up at him. He was standing looking angrily at his penis which in turn was looking morosely at me. What's that word when you can't piss in front of other people? The urinary equivalent of impotence, thank the lord? Camera-shy. That was it.

"Another thing about Westerners, Mister Arnold," he said, putting his dick away. "They fornicate, make decadent films about fornication. And they think they can teach us about society and morals." He hadn't finished. "Have you ever been in love, Mister Arnold? It is not at all comfortable, especially when you are in love with a beautiful woman. A Christian woman to boot. You lose all reason. You go mad, actually. Love is madness. Love is strange."

There was a smug, phony band in the nineteen-seventies called Doctor Hook with mullet haircuts who were as soapy as

Fairy Liquid. The colonel had stolen some of their lyrics. What a sop.

"I have done nothing wrong with your wife," I said. "She embraced me out of jubilation, in the excitement of the election campaign."

"Oh, is that the case?" he said, showing his chainsaw braces on his teeth. "She embraced you out of jubilation."

"Correct, Colonel."

Makhdoom looked at me, briefly at his thug of an aide, briefly at his watch, and then back at me. He spat slowly in the dirt and wiped his lips with the back of his hand.

"Shoot him," he said.

The colonel turned and walked towards the car.

"No, no, please."

I tried to climb out of the hole but the thug pushed me back in with his foot. There was no way I was going to get shot in this fucking hole. I was more angry than scared, and my anger matched the growing roar of something heading towards us at speed. I turned to look but we were on a bend and it was now dark. Traffic without headlights. What a novelty. I couldn't see anything. I tried again to raise my body above the parapet as the thug pulled out a pistol from his side pocket. The noise was upon us and instantly above my head and above the roar of the engine I heard a sickening thump of metal on flesh and bone before a screaming squeal of metal on metal. The aide had disappeared and I saw the dim tail lights of a tall, rickety truck weave a little before it headed on its way, tassels and bangles and other unnecessary accessories dangling and banging off the back. It was too dark to see Makhdoom's Suzuki Mehran, but it was obvious it had been hit. A sideways glance.

Silence. Then a moan. Then a rustling of trees to the right. I waited a few seconds before climbing out of the hole. It was as black as night. It was night, but still I was worried about being silhouetted against anything. For instance, I could see the lights of the truck on a bend a few hundred yards away across the valley now. I trod silently into the roadside grass and ducked down and tried to collect my thoughts. The moaning had stopped. I knew the ABC of first aid, something all shit-hot-shot foreign correspondents and flatulent desk editors get taught before they are allowed into hostile environments. Certainly the colonel and his aide had been pretty hostile. The ABC rules were to check first A for Airways, B for Breathing and C for Circulation. Or was it A for Arsehole, B for Bastard and C for Cunt? And then to turn the poor bastard on his side if he or she was in danger of throwing up and choking to death. I couldn't care if the moaning man had choked. In fact, if he was lying on his side already, I would have been happy to turn him on to his back.

I suspected it was the thug who had been hit. He had been standing in the road to shoot me and was now lying in a ditch having his eyes pecked at by a mongoose, I hoped. A bald eagle had flown off with his wig to use next nesting season and then thought better of it and spat it out from a height. But what had happened to Makhdoom? I didn't want to use my phone as a flashlight, though it occurred to me I ought to call someone. But who? Sultan? I didn't want him, or anyone, caught up in this. I would escape by foot. I was going to scarper down through the bush, hopefully meeting up with one of the jogging trails and not meeting up with the madly-in-love colonel.

CHAPTER EIGHT

I WAS BACK on the Margalla Road within twenty minutes. I hailed a passing Suzuki Mehran, jamming my knees into the back of the front seat, like supports under the wing of a single-prop plane, and headed for the Chateau Hill to get my stuff. I had to move fast.

"Can you wait for me?" I asked.

"How long?"

"Five hours?"

"Of course, sir."

"No. That was a joke. Maybe five minutes? And then we head for the Mongolian restaurant."

The driver bowed his head, scraping the ceiling as he did so.

I went through the ridiculous procedure of knocking on the gate, which I could have pushed open, and waiting for the security guard in his little box to put down his cup of tea and open up for me. I ran indoors, grabbed my key from behind the counter, ignored the manager and ran up to my room, making squishing noises and leaving wet footmarks on the stairs. I showered, dressed, throwing away my sodden shoes and trousers, packed within minutes and stopped still. That fucking noise had started again – a light tapping followed by the banging of the side of an empty van, then the kettle coming to a boil and then someone banging out a beat with his hands on a desk.

"Enough," I said.

I pulled open the door and stepped out into the hall where the pool table was. Todd's broken window was covered by board. Where was the noise coming from? You fucking bastards can't scare me now.

I opened the door to the next room angrily and noisily. Two men sat on each of the single beds facing each other. They were looking at me with wide open eyes. One had a small drum between his knees, one had a table, the third had a washing machine and the fourth an electric kettle. He touched it now by mistake and said "ouch".

"What are you doing?" I asked.

The men looked at each other, then back at me.

"We are in the process of forming a drumming and steam-hissing and singing band," the man with the burnt hand said.

"We are looking in earnest for a singer," the man straddling the washing machine said.

I was in a hurry. I had no idea what to do or say. I had never been in this situation before.

"Do you know you make a bloody racket?" I said. "All through the night, you do nothing but make a hideous noise."

"You cannot constrain the arts," the man with the burnt hand said, "with bourgeois considerations such as the time of day."

"The time of *night*," I said. "When most people are trying to sleep." You could constrain the arts, I briefly considered, any time, any place, with a couple of pipe bombs.

I closed the door gently, walked downstairs and paid the bill. I had been there too long already. I was in the back of the taxi in a jiffy.

"The Mongolian restaurant and then the airport, please," I told the driver.

But it was too good to be true. The colonel could have had the airport covered within minutes of sleepy Todd waking up, guns at the ready. Again I wondered, should I ask the driver to take me to Lahore where I could get on any plane to anywhere? I looked at the driver's face in the mirror. He looked old and wise, like a lion in a cutesy-cutesy, Hello Kitty cage for rabbits.

"Driver?" His eyes registered me slowly. "I need to fly away from Pakistan, but I don't want to fly from Islamabad."

He started to chew, looking at me every now and then as we passed a line of perhaps fifty Suzuki Mehrans lining up overnight for a tank full of compressed gas.

"Are you a fugitive from our justice system?"

"No, not all," I said. Justice system? Don't make me laugh. "To tell you the truth, it is my wife. I want to escape my wife who is flying out tonight too. From Islamabad."

"Escape your wife?"

"Correct."

"I can help you escape."

I wanted to ask if he could be a bit more specific, shocking myself yet again with that English know-it-all sarcasm. I wanted to do the right thing and let him speak in his own time. I waited. And waited. But he didn't say anything else.

"Can you be a bit more specific?" I asked.

He glanced at me in the mirror. Morose is as morose does. "How much money do you have?" he asked.

"A bit. Not much."

"Where you want to go?"

"Anywhere."

The driver raised his shoulders and turned left into an unlit side road, took a couple of turns and pulled up behind four taxis whose drivers were sitting on the curb smoking and talking. He got out and talked with them.

"Terrific," I said to myself.

The five were huddled together now in a group squat. Every now and then one would turn his head to look back at me. I was not being smart. I was entirely at their mercy. My driver stood up and walked back to the car. He leant in his window.

"Two hundred dollars and you have reservation on flight to Dubai. Time of departure: three hours."

"From where?"

"Peshawar."

"Peshawar?"

"Peshawar."

"Isn't that awfully dangerous at this time of night?"

The man stood up and said something slowly in Urdu to his mates, presumably translating what I had just said. They all had a good laugh. He leant back in the car.

"You want Peshawar?"

"Okay," I said.

"You pay for ticket at airport. You pay two hundred dollars to me."

"Okay."

He handed me a piece of paper and a pencil. "You write full name on this."

The rule was never drive at night in Pakistan unless you had to. That was one rule. Another rule was never drive around Peshawar at night, even if you had to. It was now eleven o'clock and the flight was leaving at two in the morning. Peshawar was an hour's drive, barring unforeseen events. I Googled the Dawn newspaper. No mention yet of any car accident in the Margalla Hills. No mention of any fatalities, or small soldiers with braces on their teeth.

My phone rang.

"Hadley?"

"Who is this?"

"Hadley, it's David. David Creasel."

Bloody hell, the high commissioner. "Good evening, sir."

"Good evening. Where are you?"

"Where am I? Good question, actually, sir. I am leaving."

"Good heavens. Are you in a fit condition? Colonel Makhdoom has just called me. I am afraid he is awfully upset."

So he was alive and kicking then. "Oh dear. Why is that?"

"Hadley, you should be back in hospital. You need rest. You

have been through an awful lot."

"I have been through quite a lot, sir. Yes. I have a broken tooth. Which is why I'm scarpering. The colonel tried to kill me, as it happens."

"I fear that you don't know what you are saying. Can you at least tell me where you are?"

I put my hand against the phone and told the driver which way to go. "The ring road," I said. "Approach the airport from the south." That would avoid the "shooting target" patch where, according to Sultan, the Taliban rang ahead when they saw a plum prize of a Western company's fancy SUV.

"Hadley?"

"Yes, sir."

"You are taking a ring road? Where are you taking a ring road to? I know of no ring roads. You can't escape, old chap. You do realise that, I hope."

"Sorry, sir?" Whose side was he on, for fuck's sake?

"Look, I have a friend of yours with me. And a friend of mine. Perhaps he can convince you to come home and clean up a bit and we can have a few drinks and have some fun."

"Have some fun?"

"I'm transferring the telephone to him now. Please hold on, dear fellow."

I heard a rustle and swish of material and a clunk and what appeared to strained, muted expletives between two men.

"'Ad-leh?" Oh for fuck's sake. "Why do you treat me so cruell-eh, 'Ad-leh?"

I hung up and turned off the phone.

We drove along the familiar highway, once missing a goat by yards, once missing a car reversing in the fast lane with no lights because he had missed a turn. I saw the chimneys of the brick factories against the flat, moon-lit horizon. And there was the Pearl-Continental on the right, which meant the driver had failed to take the ring road and was headed in the crazy, hubbub of downtown Peshawar. What was wrong with everyone in this country?

"Why are we going this way?"

"A swifter route."

Immediately we were caught behind a donkey and cart, and being overtaken by the brightly painted buses. Pillion passengers on motorbikes were giving me a good look as they squeezed by in the street light. How come the place was busy this late? I assumed everyone would be at home in bed.

"Put this on," the driver said, passing back a fawn-coloured woolly hat worn by almost everyone. I did as I was told and crouched down even further in the back of the cab which was making me crouch anyway.

A beggar boy selling cigarettes leant in the front window and said something, gesturing back to me with his thumb. They laughed and the boy ran off.

"What did he say?" I asked.

"No, sir, it was nothing."

"Please, I want to know. He was talking about me."

"No, really."

"What did he say?"

The driver sighed and gripped the top of the steering wheel as if bracing for a collision. "He asked me, why does that English, how you say, penis? Why does that English penis wear hat and look like dick?"

"He said that?"

"Yes. I ask him how he know you English. He said because you look like dick."

I kept silent until we reached the airport and paid the driver the two hundred dollars.

"That is for the reservation," he said. "Another hundred for me."

"But you said two hundred."

"Please, another hundred for me."

I paid him. There was no time to lose, assuming I did really have a reservation. But I was confident. The place hadn't been cordoned off and wasn't crawling with overweight soldiers. And I was in an airport, which for me has always meant hope and surprise.

I ORDERED A LARGE WHISKY about half an hour after takeoff and was cheered to see my Pakistani neighbour do the same. In fact, I said cheers. The Emirates flight attendants were being kept pretty busy down both aisles with requests for alcohol, row by row. Not so much as when the cat's away as when the mice are away. Happiness at last. Relaxation. An attendant walked past and offered me a newspaper.

"Splendid," I said.

I opened the Dawn and turned to the foreign pages.

"Oh no," I said. "Oh no."

It was a Shrubs story and it was wrong. It was about me, but it wasn't. It was about someone else. I couldn't tell. I was totally confused. But I could tell you the writer, just by the shoot-from-the-hip style. It was my old mate Fagin.

Any marina in a storm, pakistan beauty tells drunken sailor hong kong (Shrubs) – Pakistani poster child politician Marina Makhdoom left a Hong Kong club in the early hours of Sunday in the arms of a drunken Norwegian sailor, apparently set on ending her political career, Shrubs can confirm.

"Any marina in a storm," she told him breathlessly before the couple left the main bar at Rick's Cafe and headed out into the cold morning air, a reliable source and witness to the conversation said.

"He was clearly the worse for wear, but she seemed sober and knew what she was doing," the source said.

The whereabouts of Makhdoom, already criticised by many in her Muslim-majority country for being a Christian, has been the subject of speculation, on and off, since she left the family home in Lahore,

Pakistan, and went walkabout for a few days back in January.

Marina herself recently flew to Hong Kong for some well-earned R&R after appearing to suffer some sort of nervous collapse at an election rally last week in which she started spouting best-forgotten Rick Astley lyrics from the 1980s.

The Pakistani Consulate said only two days ago that she was well on her way to recovery and focusing her attention on her campaign, but that campaign appears to be in freefall.

It was full of Faginisms: "Best-forgotten Rick Astley lyrics." What a patronising fucker. What on earth was a "Pakistani poster child politician"? Who was the "reliable source"? And "Pakistan beauty"? Seriously? Her campaign "appears to be in freefall"? Said who? Since when did Shrubs go in for editorialising?

Any marina in a storm. That was my line. I told her about it on the beach. She wasn't impressed. She used those words again? I pressed the button for another drink.

"Marina Makhdoom," my middle-aged neighbour said, looking at the undated picture in the newspaper of her dancing in a London club three years earlier. "She must make up her mind whether to be the saviour of Pakistan or its shame."

I gently tore out the article, put it in my pocket. I changed planes in Dubai and got into Hong Kong around midday the next day. And as soon as I opened the red, metal door of my Tai Po home, I knew that I had had an uninvited guest.

The door opens on to stone steps leading up to a tiled hallway and at the top of the steps was something that shouldn't have been there. I live like a slob, with someone coming in just a couple of hours a week to clean up, but I generally leave the passageways clear. I could also smell a faint musk that wasn't mine or anyone's I knew. I stood at the open door, not quite sure what to do. The something was the corner of a blue box. Which blue box? There were wire-mesh screens to stop anything coming in even if I had left a window open. There was a tiny banana plantation behind the house, but the nearest trees were twenty feet away. At the front, there was a six-foot gap over a path and open drain to the ancient, one-storey house in front, with the view of a flower farm over the black tiles. This was the route Marina had taken. At the side where I was standing, there was another path, where I had seen her waiting at my door. On the opposite side, there was a pile of logs stacked against a wooden hut. In short, there was no access, with all the windows closed, except through the metal door where I was now standing, staring up the stairs. Like a berk. I decided to be bold.

"Is there anybody there?"

A bird flew out from under one of the curved red tiles. The green metal door of my Hakka neighbours opened behind me. The large, old woman carried a chicken under her arm. She grimaced at me, sat at a plastic stool and cut the bird's throat with one easy motion with a knife. The animal was shaking as if very cold as blood spilled into the open drain and ran downhill towards the flower farm. This woman rarely spoke to me. She rarely spoke to anyone. Her husband drove a green New Territories minibus and he rarely spoke to anyone either. When he came off shift, he would peel off his shirt and cough and spit several times as he made his way along the damp path from the road and toss his beer can into the woodpile.

In halting Cantonese, I asked the woman if she had seen anyone enter my flat. I had still not stepped inside.

"There is there isn't person come see me ah?" I asked, using a grammatical structure which works much better in Chinese than in English.

Her answer was concise and to the point.

"Fucking crazy ghost person."

Okay, thanks. She was talking about me, not anyone who may have come to visit me. I was white, so I looked like a ghost. Simple, really. I looked back up the stairs, hoping there weren't any crazy ghost persons up there.

I started up, my eyes on the corner of the blue box which I now saw originally contained two hundred and fifty tubes of "anti-inflammatory cream for scaly orifices such as ears, knees". I hadn't bought the cream. It was just a box I had picked up at Park 'n' Shop to carry the gin home in my Mercedes.

At the top of the stairs, I was in for a surprise. The intruder had emptied a box of soap powder all along the hall. I noticed there weren't any footprints. Pretty significant should the police have to be called.

I turned to the left and looked into the main room, ten foot square, with the view out over the flower farm. Everything seemed to be in place – the television, the iPod speakers, a camera slung over the corner of a rattan bookcase – except for one glaring thing. So glaring, in fact, that I missed it at first.

Someone had stolen the window.

Well, not someone. The window of opportunity. He was just showing off. To a soapy, soppy Brit. I called up the Shrubs person who dealt with security matters and he told me to write an email explaining exactly what had been stolen (I don't think he believed me) and why I thought it had been stolen. Easy. Well, easy-ish. Just say the fucker with the braces was mad and the fucker with the ear rings was fucking mad.

I checked each room for damage, things missing. I checked the sheets on the bed. All appeared to be in order. Next I called up my cleaner to come round to get someone to clear up the mess and fix the window and change the lock on the front door and the balcony door. Fixing the window in England would probably take a few days, if not a few weeks. In Hong Kong, in the most far-flung rural outpost of the former British colony, it would be fixed within a couple of hours.

Next priority was to have a shower and drive into town and get pissed. I had in mind Rick's Cafe in Tsim Sha Tsui, where I had first met Marina. I couldn't stop myself.

My phone went.

"Hadley?"

"Yes?"

"It's Marina."

"Marina?"

"I have to see you."

"You have to see me? I think your husband has done my flat over."

"Has he? What an antagonistic brute. I must see you. This evening."

"He stole my window."

"Hadley, I am sorry if my husband has caused you yet more sorrow, but I must insist on seeing you."

"Where?"

And here was the strange thing. She wanted to meet at an address in Tai Po, less than a mile from my house. It was the top floor of a thin block of flats above a Chinese bank I had never heard of. She said she was waiting for me.

I parked outside a restaurant where black and yellow snakes lay coiled in round, wire baskets stacked on top of each other on the pavement. I waved to the minibus driver – my neighbour! – who sat waiting for a full load of passengers before heading across the stinking Lam Tsuen River and into the green and lush Lam Tsuen Valley and past my village. He ignored me. I passed the watch shop and the gold shop and found the Chinese bank. I pressed 36A which had a yellow Post-it note stuck above it with Sellotape saying "Last Dance Saloon". Curious. The door buzzed and I opened the metal grille. An old man wearing a vest and shorts sat behind a desk, listening to a large transistor radio with an earphone. He did not register my existence. Terrific security, I thought. What on earth was Marina doing in a place like this?

The lift was one square metre. How did people move furniture in and out of upper flats, something as ordinary as a reasonably sized chest of drawers or a piano? What happened when someone died? Did they prop them up in the corner? A chain rattled at every floor as the lift rose slowly to the top.

I knocked at the door of 36A, where "Last Dance Saloon" was hand-written in bigger letters on a piece of A4 paper. A dapper young Chinese man opened the door, grinning broadly and stepping back to let me in. He was wearing an expensive grey silk suit over a tee-shirt.

"You must be Hadley," he said. A right toff.

"Yes, I had a message..."

"From my sister, yes. She is expecting you."

"Your sister?"

"Indeed yes. She's just popped out to get some fags." A right toff who liked to slum it every now and then with his vocabulary.

"I see."

"Please come in and take a seat."

I walked into a large sitting room, two rooms knocked into one, with the standard parquet flooring, a mirror and rail along one wall, a piano at one end and a reasonably sized chest of drawers at the other. Above the chest was a window looking east out over the tat of the new town on to the Tai Po waterfront park and the blue waters of Plover Cove, the lighter blue hills of Sai Kung in the distance. The only other furniture was three wooden school chairs.

"This is a dance studio," I said stupidly, sitting down.

"Yes, that is correct," the man said, pulling a chair round to sit opposite me and putting out his hand. "Sorry, I am Sebastian."

"Sebastian?"

"Yes. I am Marina's half brother. This is my business. Dancing. I understand you are a journalist?"

"Yes. I got to know your sister in Pakistan."

"I know all about it. She won't be a tick. Can I get you a cup of tea?"

"No thank you."

"Something stronger? A Black Label, for instance?"

"That would be wonderful. Please."

"Marina said you were a lush." Sebastian slapped his knees, rose from the chair and headed into the kitchen.

"Oh, right."

"Give him a Scotch and he'll be a happy man, she said," he called back. "You must have so many questions."

"I had no idea Marina had a brother."

"A-ha. I have no qualms in telling you of my provenance, Hadley. Marina has assured me of your integrity." He stood in the kitchen doorway. "My father, Marina's father, had a relationship with a smoking hot Chinese dancer when he was posted here with the consulate decades ago. Hence me. Hence the dance."

Sebastian disappeared again and I heard the wonderful clinking of ice and glasses. I clapped my hands silently. He returned with a tray.

"Is it public knowledge, about you and your sister?"

He put the tray on the third chair and poured me a triple.

"No, not exactly," he said. "I have used my family connections to get this place off the ground, but no one knows about those connections." He was looking around him as though this were the Royal Ballet School, not a three-hundred-square-foot apartment in what many in the West would consider a crawling, high-rise slum.

"Those were the days," he said. "Did you know I once met Anthony Newley?"

"Wow."

"We were like brothers."

I was trying to do the arithmetic in my head. I imagined an age gap, if Tony Newley were still alive, of about seventy years. He could have been like Mian Langhari's brother, but surely not Sebastian's.

"Where did you meet him?"

"Here."

"He came to see you in this flat?"

"He was a friend of my father. He wanted the publicity

surrounding his visit to help my business, being the finest British dancer and all-round entertainer."

"And did it help?"

"We closed the next day."

"What rotten luck."

I heard the latch on the door.

"There she is. But then I reopened. Tap dance mainly, but the neighbours complained about the noise. So my students wear socks."

Marina came in carrying two Park 'n' Shop carrier bags, a big smile on her un-made-up face, her hair done up in a bun held together by a pencil.

"Hello again, Hadley."

We shook hands. "The last time I saw you..." I began.

"...was in front of all those people," she said. "Before I had my turn."

"Your turn, yes."

"Before you had your fall. I trust you are fully recovered?"

"Yes, I am fine thank you. Your husband put paid to one of my teeth, but that's a different story."

"I shall look forward to hearing all details. Bring your drink on to the roof. Sebastian has a lesson coming up."

We walked through the narrow kitchen and out a side door on to the roof. Each tiny top-floor flat – penthouse was too posh a word – had its own area, and Sebastian's was fenced off from its neighbours with a gap showing the view of Plover Cove and Sai Kung. There was expensive outdoor furniture and a barbecue. We sat at a circular table, under a giant white umbrella.

"Thanks for coming, Hadley. I am happy to renew our acquaintance."

I briefly wondered about her security people and whether they were looking at us now. Or whether Todd and the colonel were listening in, smoking and sharing an earphone between them in the back of a Suzuki Mehran. I briefly wondered how anyone could lead a life like this. So duplicitous and phony, surrounded by so many dangerous people.

"Your brother gives tap lessons to students who wear socks," I said. "Because of the noise."

"Correct," Marina said. "Occasionally, when the weather is clement, they will go to the waterside. That is a more satisfactory arrangement."

"I see. Very strange. Your husband broke my tooth and hurt me in a dentist's chair. He ordered a man to kill me in a drain on the Margalla Hills and I believe he stole my living room window."

"I am afraid that would not be the first such occurrence."

"They were all first such occurrences for me. He dropped me in a hole and tried to urinate on my head." I found myself tapping the table top. "None of this seems to take you by surprise."

She pulled out a cigarette and lit it without offering one to me. I took a long slug of the Scotch. All irritation vanished. She went back inside, brought out the tray of drinks and poured herself a gin and tonic.

"I can't keep apologising for my husband," she said. "He can be brutal. The reason I asked you to come over is to discuss an idea I and my advisers have been considering."

She stubbed out her cigarette, reached into her handbag and brought out an almost-normal-sized spliff.

"If I am to become a successful politician..." She lit the joint and did one of her sudden Hoover-like inhalations and spoke as though without vocal chords. "...I must put away childish things. Fuck me, this is good stuff."

"Sorry, I don't quite understand."

"It is a reference to Shakespeare."

"As in, 'fuck me, sweet prince, this is good stuff'?"

"No..."

"You mean you must choose between being a good king or hanging out with whores and riff-raff. You are choosing to be the good king."

She leant forward and touched my hand. "Exactly."

"What childish things did you have in mind?"

"That is the key. You want to try some of this?"

I took the joint between thumb and forefinger. "If you want to become prime minister...." I took a deep hit with a loud, inward "ooof" noise and finished the sentence as though I had been stabbed in the neck: "...you should convert to Islam."

"You've read my mind," she said, taking back the joint. She did a quick inhalation with a sort of a double-take catching of her breath, licking her lips. "There are many newspapers in Pakistan that would write stories about how I had grown up and was giving up Christianity but no one would believe them, for they are all partisan. You know this. But if Shrubs were to write the same story, if you were to write the same story, to show your gratitude, the world would sit up and take notice. The Pakistani people would take notice."

"You mean, write that you are giving up alcohol, drugs, partying and Christianity?"

"If you wrote that story for me... To give it some gravitas. Not just my announcement, but the suggestion that it is true. It would take the heat off you as far as my husband and his cronies are concerned. That I can guarantee. There would be another bonus."

"What's that?"

"Simply that, without anyone having to know, I would let you kiss me."

The sun was dropping quickly, reflecting brightly in my eyes off a window in the next building.

"I see," I said. "You mentioned gratitude."

"Correct," she said.

"I apologise in advance if I am being rude, but gratitude for what exactly?"

A piano struck up indoors. It was "The Candy Man Can", by Tony Newley, a mawkish, fanciful, festering song popular with paedophiles the world over. Marina took another hit.

"You think that monster of a man in the Margalla Hills was run over by accident?"

"You mean..."

"... Someone was attentively watching your back, yes. Now will you do this small thing for me?"

"You mean..."

"I am not going to breathe another word about it. About the hit and run. And neither are you. This is how you can thank me."

"I don't know what to say," I said. "Words aren't enough."

"Not spoken words, no. Written ones would be appropriate."

Was it possible? That huge, unwieldy truck with no lights? How could they have seen anything? In the land of 1945 Hoovers, Bakelite electrical fittings and mid-sixties Goblin Teasmades, they had thermal imaging binoculars?

"Tell me, Marina, what happened to you that night in Lahore? At the campaign rally."

"What do you think happened? I was affected and emotional, obviously. But I was also proving a point. It matters not what I say at campaign rallies." She nailed the end of the joint into the ashtray and downed her G&T in one. "The lesson has begun. You must go."

Inside, about twenty children were lined up ready to dance. They looked dolefully at us in the mirror, as if to say what's the fucking point of doing this in socks? Sebastian waved and kept playing. Marina saw me out to the lift.

"I shall be in touch," she said.

"Thank you. Indeed. From the bottom..."

"Please give some thought to my request. A nice story, written by a nice man."

Oh right. Nice one.

CHAPTER NINE

"Hadley, I will let you explain what's happened with Marina Makhdoom," Baxter said. "Where we stand with the story at this point in time and what we can go with. First off, and I apologise if I have missed something, but in all this drama, you don't seem to have written anything. Not one word."

"I can explain that," I said. I was in the office the next morning with Baxter, Fagin and the chief security guy who was appalled that I hadn't reported the dentist/manhole/penis waving/ death threat incidents earlier. "I wanted to contextualise the information first."

"What did you just say?" Baxter asked. "You wanted to *contextualise the information?* What the fuck does that mean?"

"I wanted to pull together all the strands."

"What are you talking about? This is a news agency, not a trouser repair shop. We write news and put it out immediately. We brush in relevance and background, but we don't contextualise anything. You're fucking mad."

"Hadley did try to give me one story," Fagin said. "When he first found Makhdoom. It was the middle of the night. I told him to hold off."

"To contextualise it. Exactly. Then the consulate came out with her being in Hong Kong, which kind of killed it," I said. "They scooped me."

"Sorry, Hadley," Fagin said.

"It's nothing."

"And since then?" Baxter asked. "The dentist, the manhole, the cricket roller, the killing...?"

"I had been threatened, Rodney. She and I were in danger. Are in danger. The fucking colonel told me not to breathe a word. What was I supposed to do?"

"Tell me. That is what you should have done. Immediately, for fuck's sake. And now you have this secret meeting in Tai Po. What was all that about?"

"She told me she had some interesting news."

"Again, I don't see any story. What is the news, Hadley? Why are you being so coy? What did she say?"

"Well it's difficult. She told me this amazing stuff. It is just so sensitive."

"Tell us."

"She said she had erred."

"Sorry?"

"She said she had erred in her ways and needed to repent." There was silence around the room. "She said she had done bad things, the drink, the drugs, the affairs, and if she wanted a fair crack at becoming a successful politician, she had to change."

"So far, PR bollocks," Fagin said. "What else?"

"Indeed. She said she had to convert to Islam."

"What?"

"She used Shakespeare. She quoted Prince Hal saying she had to give up childish things to become king."

"For fuck's sake. What are you talking about?"

"She wants to convert to Islam so she can become prime minister. That's how I read it."

They all looked at one another across the table. "That's better," Baxter said. "She will let you write that?"

"Yes."

"But how do we know she isn't just playing us?"

"How do you mean?"

"Well, it is the PR bollocks that Fagin just mentioned. She has

Pakistan papers that love her. Why doesn't she turn to them?"

"She said something about integrity. The integrity of Shrubs."

"But Hadley, we mustn't set ourselves up for a fall. It is all very well saying she has vowed to do these things. But that is all it is so far. Words."

"I think she really means it. I mean, I know she really means it."

"That is all very well and good, but we would have to introduce the voice of scepticism. You would agree with that, right? A balancing comment. She is, after all, borderline crazy, right?"

They were correct. But just as I couldn't buy completely into Marina's version of events, nor could I buy into theirs. Had she really saved my life? Baxter and Fagin looked at each other.

"Hadley, laddie," Fagin began. "Has this wee nutter turned your head?"

"How do you mean?"

"Well to us sitting here, Marina Makhdoom appears to be a political lightweight, whose apparent crush on Rick Astley has made her spoiled goods."

"She was under a lot of pressure. She had been smoking."

"She gave you a wee embrace on the stage."

"I can't help that."

"Has she made you an offer you can't refuse?"

"Don't be ridiculous." A kiss she had said. Hot Chocolate said it started with a kiss.

"Hadley. Open your eyes. Look at her track record. She is a mawkish, self-indulgent, arrogant and hugely rich young beauty, who has screwed everyone from Henry Kissinger to Mian Langhari."

"Henry Kissinger?" It started with a Kissinger.

"She is also about to start campaigning, as you would have us believe, as a born-again Muslim, giving up sex and drugs and rock and roll. Seriously?"

Baxter swung round from his view out over the harbour.

"Hadley, I'm taking you off the story."

"What?"

"My mind's made up. You are far too close to it all. You have been through too much and become emotionally involved. Fagin's right. She is a piece of fluff, though of course there is a story in her even suggesting she wants to convert to Islam."

"I agree. I can write that. I just don't think we should trash her."

Fagin shrugged his shoulders. Of course they were right, the bastards. What was I playing at? It was her pants, that was all. Her pants had turned my head.

"You are correct of course," I said. "Let me try to talk to her again."

"No need for that. Hand over all your notes to Fagin."

"I haven't got any notes."

"You didn't take notes?"

"No. I wasn't thinking. But I can see her again. Any time."

"Any place," Fagin said.

"You don't think there's a story there at all, do you?" I said to Fagin.

"Nothing that you should get involved with, no."

I MET FAGIN in the Foreign Correspondents' Club, after fighting my way from Central MTR station through the yellow-clad student protesters and up Wyndham Street and the fifty-four steps of the Ice House stairway to the club entrance. I arrived panting and leant on the wall for a few seconds to allow the blotches on my face to die down. The FCC, a brown and white colonial-era building which used to be an ice house, is my favourite place to drink, if the time is right and it is empty. Early evenings from Monday to Thursday are fine. The place has to be avoided on Friday nights, New Year's Eve, or any obscure British festivals when lawyers and bankers wear silly clothes, accompany silly people, and generally piss off the one or two members who are actually correspondents.

It was five-thirty on a Tuesday evening and the main bar was deserted. Perfect. I ordered a large gin and tonic, sat at my favourite end and read the South China Morning Post as I waited for Fagin who turned up twenty minutes later wearing a kilt.

"What are you doing?" I asked.

"It's Burns Night, you prick."

"Burns Night? That's in January."

"Aye, but the place was closed for renovation, if you remember. And the events calendar was full up. So they chose tonight."

"But that means all these people will come in wearing kilts and playing bagpipes."

"Piping the haggis, aye. It's great."

"Well how much time do we have?"

"How much time?"

"Before people start behaving like children and looking up each other's kilts and shitting in ashtrays."

"The main programme shouldn't get going until about eight."

"All right. What are you having to drink?"

"A large Black Label, thanks. And talking about behaving like children."

"What's that supposed to mean?"

"Well what was that show you were putting on for Baxter? Are you in love, laddie?"

"I admitted he was right, didn't I?"

"Aye, but it was obviously a half-hearted change of heart."

"It just seems to me that we are all too willing to bury her. What was that story you wrote about her being picked up by a drunken sailor?"

"What about it?"

"Well, who was your source? You used that line I told you about. 'Any marina in a storm'. Except I told you 'any port in a storm', if I remember correctly. Who was your source? Who said 'marina' and not 'port'."

"Hadley, calm down."

"Tell me who your source was. No one knew about that line. Only Marina. She would never have used it."

"Are you shagging her?"

"Fuck off, Fagin. Whoever your source was played you for a fool. She never said that."

"The manager saw her leave with the sailor."

"And he heard her say that line?"

"No, that was someone else."

"Who? I can tell you who. Someone out to hurt her."

"If you must know, it was a senior aide to her husband."

"With sparkly ear rings and a daft Yorkshire accent."

"Aye, that's him."

"For fuck's sake. He is the man who wants me to be his servant."

"I'm sorry?"

"Yorkshire Todd. He had me using a vacuum cleaner and cleaning dishes and dusting fucking Venetian blinds. He's fucking mad. He's played you something rotten."

"He's played *me*, Hadley?"

"I am afraid so."

"Have you shagged her?"

Here was the thing, and it's shameful. I didn't want to have to say I hadn't shagged her. How pathetic is that?

"Here's the thing," I said.

"What thing? Either you've shagged her or not. Has she said she will shag you if you write that puff piece about her? That's it, isn't it?"

"For fuck's sake, Fagin."

"For fuck's sake, what? Of course, she wouldn't be that crude, would she? Did she say she would let you hold her hand, or kiss her on the cheek?"

Oh boy. "Remember when she went missing and the consulate

put out a story she was seeing a sick relative or something in Hong Kong?"

"I do."

"Remember I had seen her the night before? On the beach? Some prick had knocked her down at Rick's and I picked her up and we went down to Shek O."

"You shagged her on the beach?"

I signalled for another drink. "Fagin, I know so much about her. I know what she gets up to."

"Did you give her one?"

"Her husband tortured me. He's threatened me and her." I felt my eyes well up. "I haven't shagged her. But he thinks I have."

"Okay, steady."

Fagin put his hand on my shoulder and I recoiled. I wasn't used to such affection, especially from a Scottish git.

"She saved my life, Fagin."

"What?"

"When the truck came and killed the man. She said that was her people."

"Oh lord."

"Indeed. She told me not to tell anyone."

"Aye, no need to worry."

"The thing is, Baxter's right. I do have such great stories to tell. Makhdoom's top aide is barking mad. He wants me to be his servant, to clean up after him. The colonel's a dentist and uses a mallet. The future of Pakistan, of nuclear-armed Pakistan, is not in safe hands."

"What are you going to do?"

"I don't know. I've been taken off the story, right? I don't suppose I will ever see her again."

THREE NIGHTS LATER, I was back at Rick's Cafe. I installed myself in my usual seat in the corner, away from the dance floor. It was the grown-up's equivalent of the kitchen at student parties.

"Long time, Hadley," the Glaswegian manager said, putting a large gin and tonic in front of me. "The last time I saw you, you were escorting some Pakistani beauty up the stairs."

"The secret's out of the bag, then?"

"Aye. And more. We all heard about the bomb blast. We all put two and two together."

"No, you shouldn't."

"I won't then. But you're okay?"

I was getting misty-eyed, for fuck's sake. "Yes, thanks," I said.

And that was that. Scottish integrity. John Knox had it in spades. Mary Queen of Scots said as much.

Some straggling protesters, mostly gweilo and carrying yellow umbrellas, came in looking worse for wear. As did I when I looked solemnly at myself in the mirror between two bottles of Gordon's gin. I looked to the left. Oh lord. A lawyer was smirking at me. What was it this time? He headed in my direction with the smile fast turning to a "why you bastard" kind of look. I knew for sure this one was a lawyer because I had seen him pissing in a flower bed at the end of the road about a year ago.

"Are you the journalist?" he asked. "Our man in Hong Kong, that sort of thing? Is that you?"

"I am a copy editor," I said politely. "How can I help?"

"Help," he said. "That's a laugh. The reason I came over here is to find out why you people always write in sound bites?"

"I..."

"Why do you have to wait until the tenth or twentieth anniversary before you quote people saying what a sin it was to invade Iraq?" He leant towards me. "You spend a couple of weeks in a war zone and wear it on your sleeve for the rest of your lives. It's pathetic. You make me sick."

I was happy to have someone to talk to. "Tell me," I said, "don't you think lawyers should be able to charge for offering their opinions in their free time?"

Rumpole swayed gently on his heels and looked at the ceiling.

He had a very red face.

"Yes," he said. "That will be five hundred dollars."

"That's very good." Wait a minute. I had a flashback to that night. The lawyers with the moustaches like greased string. Except this one... This one had shaved. "Aren't you the prick..."

Someone came up behind me to finish the question.

"...who ran straight into me and knocked me on to the floor right on this very spot and then ran away like a felon? A blaggard?"

And before the dickhead could get his louche mouth around the word "blaggard", Marina did something that made a scraping noise like metal on bone and made me wince. She stamped down on the front of the prick's shin, using the outside rim of a highly specialised shoe. It was a less subtle version of Rosa Klebb's poison-laced dagger in "From Russia With Love". It tore a six-inch hole in expensive worsted cotton, drew lashings of blood and reduced the lawyer to a heap.

"Come on, Hadley," she said, leaving a thousand dollar note on the bar and pulling me towards the stairs. "Let's hit the boulevard."

I signalled to the Glaswegian manager with a couple of glances between him and the money that there was probably some change due the next time I saw him and followed Marina out the building. It was only at the top of the stairs I realised she was wearing dark glasses, just like the first time we had met. She stood staring at me, and me at her. She took off the glasses to reveal the wet eyes, glistening under the blue, green and orange neon of a circular sign saying "Welcome to Rick's". She leant forward and kissed my lips softly, and for a good three seconds. She stepped back, ever so slightly panting.

"Probably best you don't tell anyone about this," she said.

"Tell anyone about what?"

"Come on, I want to show you something."

I recognised the line straight away. It was Julia Roberts talking to Hugh Grant after she kissed him for the first time in "Notting Hill". What a fucking phony! We turned right into the white noise and lights of Carnarvon Road's camera shops, Vietnamese, Cantonese and Korean restaurants, money changers, massage parlours on high floors, shops selling Chinese leather pilots' briefcases, people standing in doorways offering anything and everything in hushed voices. Someone offered Marina a fake Rolex and escaped the shoe thing.

There, parked on a double yellow line and guarded by a man in uniform, was a white, open-top BMW, about the same vintage as my Mercedes but in tip-top condition. Tip-top was the kind of expression Marina would use.

The guard handed Marina the key and she told me to hop in. She gunned the engine, lifted her sunglasses on to her hair, bit her bottom lip and did not as much as given a token glance in the rear-view mirror as the car took off.

"Where are we going?" I asked.

"You'll see."

I was seriously concerned. The woman was troubled, to say the least. She had been drinking and she was behind the wheel. I did up my seatbelt and gripped the door with my left hand and the bottom of my seat with my right.

"Relax, Hadley."

I can't stand people telling me to relax. It all began with that line: "Probably best you don't tell anyone about this." She was a complete fake.

We passed a building where I had pissed in the lobby years before, thinking it was condemned. The building looked derelict, then and now, its paintwork pitted with mould. It was in fact prime property and, new to Hong Kong and drunk, I had jumped to the first of many wrong conclusions. Now it was being torn down. A huge, red cloth sign said yet another shopping centre was to take its place. It didn't say "yet another". Those are my words.

"I hate the mall," Marina said, ramming the gear lever into second.

"I'm sorry?" I said, but my voice was drowned out by the noise of the traffic. The conversation was over.

She took the harbour tunnel back to Hong Kong island and was following the same route to Shek O we had taken the first night. The air cooled as we climbed the hill, the smell of the moist vegetation taking me back to childhood holidays in Essex, and still she wouldn't speak. She took the bends too fast as we headed down into the village, leaning into corners instead of changing gear. Before the right turn through the golf course towards the Thai restaurant and the sea, she slowed and turned left into the drive of one of the huge houses looking down on the village. The name of the house, caught in the headlights on a brass plaque, was "Margalla Hills".

The gates opened automatically. Marina drove up a hill, rhododendron bushes on each side, the lights showing a large, three-storey white house with eaves and blue window frames. There was a lawn to the left and a turreted courtyard and garage to the right into which she drove, pulling up inches before a workbench a foot deep in spanners, hammers, hoses, saws, half a lawnmower, two vices and paraffin cans. Wooden planes hung from the walls.

"Here we are," she said, patting my knee. "I've given the staff the night off. It's just you and me."

We walked across the lawn and I thought I could hear the sea crashing against rocks. The door was unlocked. I followed her into a damp-smelling corridor. She turned on the lights and led me into a sitting room full of rosewood furniture and two white, rattan sofas. A bit like my own, actually.

"Sit," she said. "I shall make you a gin and tonic as I know you like it."

I sat on the sofa facing the window. She came back with the drinks and sat next to me. She was brim-full of energy. It struck me that she might be bi-polar. She was manic and earnest. Like a CNN reporter.

"You may wonder what you are doing here," she said.

"Well..."

"The truth of the matter is that you make me feel comfortable, Hadley."

"That's good."

"Yes. It's first class. Whenever I am in public and am thinking of you, I shall do this." She put her drink on the table, sat back, raised her arms and rested her long, downward-pointing finger tips on the top of her head. "I am making a heart with my arms and hands. Do you see it?"

"Yes," I said. "You told us this in Lahore." Completely barmy.

"But I am not talking to a group of journalists now. I am talking to you. It is a gesture of the affection I have for you. A first-class gesture." She reached for her bag and brought out a spliff.

"Oh, it's another huge one."

"So many men want sex and no affection. So it is with me. I am like those men. And when I find a man for whom I have affection..." She looked at me through fucking tears. "I am hoping for encouraging news about the little story you are writing about me." She put her hand on my knee. "How it is going to put my political career on the correct rails." She was marking a track with her fingers on my knee.

"Well it's funny you should mention that," I said. "I had a word with my colleagues and they think it's a great story."

"First class."

"But we would have to have balancing comment."

"Balancing comment?"

"Well, yes. A comment from someone, a political opponent, saying what he thinks about your plan. Whether it would work. Whether or not it's too late to turn your career around."

"Well, that's not very nice."

Her hand had stopped.

"This is how it works, Marina. You know that."

"I had hoped you might be showing more gratitude."

"I am grateful, Marina. But there is nothing I can do. I have been taken off the story, anyway. They say I am too close."

"Too close?"

"So much has happened to me. I think they are thinking in terms of post traumatic stress syndrome."

"Post dramatic...? What is that please?"

The manic earnestness had been replaced by cutesy pouting. I reached inside my jacket pocket and pulled out the crumpled cutting of Fagin's "Pakistani poster child politician" article. Humans are the only primates that can derive pleasure from hurting one of their kind.

"I read this on the plane," I said, holding it limply before her. "Did you see it?"

She took it from my hands. She stared at it, her lips apart.

"You said 'any marina in a storm' to a Norwegian sailor," I said. "That was my line to you."

She put the cutting on the table. "You don't understand how these things work," she said.

"I think I do, Marina."

"No. You see, someone told a lie to the reporter. It is not very unusual in my country. Someone pays someone to pay someone to introduce a story. Everyone is conspiring to bring down everyone, one way or the other, if they're not having them softly killed. And someone has told a lie about me and you believe it."

"Was he Norwegian?"

"What of it? I was with a sincere and kindly man."

"The other part of the story, I am led to believe, was provided by Todd, your husband's aide."

"It would not surprise me. He is violent and depraved to infinity, as I believe I have already told you. I am going to tell you something that will make you feel more clearly about me."

"Clearly. That would be good."

"A long time ago, an American president came on to me in the Oval Office bathroom. And a French president."

"On separate occasions, I assume."

Marina leant back against the sofa and put her hands in the air, stretching her blouse over her breasts. "And several world famous entertainers and sportsmen – at least four cricketers from your country," she said.

I thought briefly of Geoffrey Boycott, with an accent not unlike Yorkshire Todd, as Marina put her hand on her heart and puckered her lips in a kind of spoilt-baby "don't be mean to me" expression. If I had seen this in a movie, I would have snarled "for fuck's sake" under my breath and repositioned myself in my seat.

She went on: "The point I am trying to make..."

She was cut short. Headlights swept across the curtains and ceiling as a car came up the drive and Marina put her hands to her mouth.

"For fuck's sake," I said. "What is it now?"

"I am fearing it is time for you to go."

She was fearing? I was fearing. I didn't know who I was more afraid of, Yorkshire Todd or the colonel. I followed Marina to the window, three steps behind.

"He mustn't see you."

"Who is it?" I said. The car, a low-hung sports model, stopped in the drive and the lights went out. A man climbed out under the light of the porch, next to a brass model cannon used as a shoe scraper. He climbed quite slowly, holding on to the door frame. It was Mian Langhari.

"Has he hurt his back?" I asked.

"Shhh."

"You were expecting him?"

"I wasn't sure. He mustn't see you. It would spoil everything. Come this way."

"I don't want to spoil everything. But he'll probably need to stop for a wee on the way to the front door."

"He is a lion of a man."

She took me by the hand and led me to a door with steps going down to a cellar.

"You are going to lock me in the cellar?"

"Do not be outrageous." She pulled me down in blackness and hit a light switch. A bare bulb lit up a room about twenty foot square with whitewashed brick walls propping up three Chinese Flying Pigeon bicycles with sprung saddles and rod brakes. "There's so little time."

"So little time for what? Marina, can't we go back upstairs again?"

"You take the bicycle and you travel that way," she said.

"Through the door?"

"Yes."

"What's through the door? I don't want to travel that way, Marina. I want to stay with you. I don't want to cycle around the cellar."

"You have to go."

"Please. You tell the old man he has to go." That was close to a Jim Reeves line. It was also the Groucho Marx line in reverse. Rejection is a huge turn on.

"There are bicycle clips on the handlebars," she said. "For your trousers."

"Marina. Please."

"I have no time to explain. I must go. Ride that way."

"I don't want to ride that way."

"Cycle for five minutes. At the end you will see a TV screen. Watch until you hear me tell you what to do next. No, there is not enough time. When you see the screen, you will see a red button on your right. Press the button and you will get a new vision on your screen. A split-screen of two roads. If the roads are clear, press the red button once again and the door will open and you will be free."

"I don't know what you are talking about." I heard the doorbell upstairs. "Your instructions are so complicated."

"Try to remember. Do not push the red button if you can see someone."

"Just tell him to go. He must be seventy-five."

"Fare thee well, Hadley."

"Fare me well? Wait, Marina. Don't go…" The door closed and she turned a key. Never trust an old man who reeks of charm, I thought.

And what was that about bicycle clips? I lifted up the bike nearest me and bounced it a couple of times. It was heavy and unwieldy and had just one gear. And this used to be a status symbol in China.

I opened the door and a light went on automatically. Then another and another, down a tunnel which curved to the right on a slight downward incline about a hundred yards ahead. It was the same height as a subway tunnel, but about half the width, and arched with red bricks which looked a century old. There was a single-bulb light behind a wire mesh every twenty paces or so. I struggled a bit getting the bike through the door which had a spring hinge. I put on the bicycle clips. I was wearing a brand new pair of cotton twill trousers and the bike, for some reason, was missing its chain guard. I had once done a story about Flying Pigeons, how they only came in black and were once the most popular form of transport on Earth, a symbol of Communist peace and harmony that would last a lifetime. I wasn't feeling very harmonious right then. Anyway, I straddled the large, hard saddle and was off.

This was fun. The tunnel sloped gently, curving to the right all the way. I stuck my legs out horizontally and made a "woo" sound, Marina all but forgotten. What had the tunnel been built for? Smuggling? Some waxy old nineteenth century Brit taipan was probably having an affair with a village girl with bound feet and brought in the builders so that a night of nooky was downhill all the way.

"Why do you keep going down to the cellar with a bottle of gin under your arm, dear?" his powdered wife, dressed in layers of black robes over layers of corsets, would have asked him.

"Just getting my leg over, darling. With a simply splendid young lass in the village. I built this tunnel, you see..."

I reached the end and parked the bike next to three others propped up against the wall. I pressed the red button as instructed. Two TV screens showed dimly lit streets outside and there was no one in sight. I hit the red button again.

Nothing happened. I tried again. Still nothing.

"You have to press it assiduously."

The voice made me jump. It was Marina, on both TV screens, a drink in her hand.

"Sorry?"

"You have to increase the pressure," she said.

"Can I come back and see you now? Has he gone?"

"He is in the lavatory."

"Of course he is. Marina..."

"Safe travels."

The screens both switched back to the two views of the streets. There was a man walking slowly, his head lowered. I waited until he had gone.

I pressed the button long and hard this time and a spring sprung and part of the wall retracted. I jumped out and the wall quickly moved back into place.

I was at the corner house where Marina had disappeared that night. There was no sign anywhere, in this light anyway, that there was a door. There was even a "keep out" warning sign stuck on the plaster over the where the door met the wall. I looked closer. It was impossible to tell where the join was.

"It says keep out."

Again I jumped. The man had reappeared, the same nutter who had told me about his dog being covered in ticks.

"Did you ever find the young Pakistani woman you were looking for?" he asked.

"You have a good memory," I said. "I did, as a matter of fact. Thanks."

"You appear to have appeared out of nowhere."

"An old party trick."

"Oh how jolly," the man said. "I love a good party. A good sing-a-long."

"Do you? That's nice. How's your dog, by the way? Baxter."

"My dog?"

"You said he was covered in ticks."

"Oh, yes. I had him shot."

No more tick problem then. "I'm very sorry to hear that," I said.

"Yes, well, it's after midnight. I have to do the laundry."

"Indeed."

I walked round the corner to the Thai restaurant, sat down and ordered a beer. Four tables in front of me sat a man smoking a cigarette, his back towards me. There was something about the posture and the army haircut. By the time I had reached Palakorn's table, my thoughts were spinning in crop circles. I was sitting down, noticing at turns that the handsome snappers' snapper was both sheepish and smug.

I hated the term "snapper" for two reasons. One, it was too close to "sniper", with all its military connotations that so many in the business loved; and two, it applied to Palakorn. I had a vision of him in bed with Marina. It was an image I managed to erase by conjuring up an image of him drowning at sea, Goblin Teasmades tied to each limb.

He shrugged his shoulders as if he could read my mind.

"There's obviously no point in trying to lie about it," he said.

"Lie about what?"

"My being here when I should be in Pakistan."

"Why are you here? You've gone AWOL. You could lose your

job."

"Yes, Hadley. I don't care. Sorry."

There was another cigarette burning in the ashtray.

"You have company," I said.

Palakorn smiled. "Gary," he said. "You just missed him. He saw you talking to the old geezer and scarpered."

"Why? I have never met Gary. What's he doing away from Islamabad? And how did he know it was me?"

"I told him."

"So..." I was so confused. "You saw me and told Gary, 'that's him' and he said 'oh shit, I've got to run'. Is that how it went?"

"More or less. He's going through difficult times."

"Is he? I'm sorry." I sat down on a round Formica stool. "Why isn't he in Pakistan?"

Palakorn shrugged again.

"I've just come from her house," I said.

"On that cool underground golf cart, I know."

"Golf cart? I came by bicycle."

"Oh."

"I didn't see any golf cart."

"Maybe it's in use."

"But why you?"

"What do you mean?"

"Why did she drive me here at the same time she is seeing you? And fucking Mian Langhari. And Gary? Is she seeing Gary?"

Palakorn's fine features were smug again. "I can't answer for him, Hadley."

"I don't know why I asked. Are you off to see her now?"

"I am. But it seems that Langhers got there before me."

"Langhers?"

"Mian."

"You call him Langhers?"

"All his mates do."

"You're his mate?"

"We got to know each other in Islamabad. He's a terrific guy."

"But Palakorn, it's all so unfair. I came down to Shek O, in her car, because she wanted to be with *me*."

"She's very accommodative."

"Accommodative? Is that all you can say?"

"Fickle, then. It's not my fault, Hadley. She came on to me."

I stared out over the roundabout, at the ads for Coke and the "Chinese and Thai Seafood Restaurant", with a man holding a giant pair of chopsticks. "She took me to this crazy bar in Islamabad where there was a back room," Palakorn said.

"A back room?"

"What's the matter?"

"I never saw any back room."

Palakorn was squeezing the cigarette between his fingers. His legs were shaking like that prat of a lawyer in Islamabad.

"Look, Hadley. I'm in love."

"Oh lord, here we go."

"I don't mind telling you so. I am not going to go into tawdry details. I know there are others. But this feeling, when you're in love with a beautiful woman..."

"Oh don't start."

"It's like a madness. Nothing else matters. My job, my friendships. I can't think of anything else."

"Well, you had better start thinking of your mate Langhers and what he's up to."

"He's very old. He won't be long."

"What?"

"They've had a thing for years. She realises there's no future in it."

"What are you saying? They've had a thing for years. She's crazy about him."

"She's going to end it. That's why I'm here. She's going to end it tonight."

"And start a thing with you?" I slapped the table and rose

from my seat. "Well good luck with that."

"Where are you going?"

"Wanchai."

"So you're done here, then?"

"I am done here, yes. I am going to go to a bar and fall in love with a beautiful woman. And then I will be done there."

CHAPTER TEN

I TOLD BAXTER everything there was to tell. About Makhdoom and Yorkshire Todd. I told him precise details of the dental treatment and the manhole and the snooker game and the percussion band and apologised profusely for not briefing him earlier. I told him about the creepy high commissioner and, lastly, about Marina. I said it was fine with me that I was off the case. I said I didn't want to write anything about Marina or Pakistan and that, if I still had a job, I was serious about wanting to write about tea.

"You've had a narrow escape there, I reckon," he said. I had been forgiven, it seemed.

"Well, you may want to haul Palakorn in and have a word in his ear. He's falling in love with the daft woman. And Gar-eh."

"Gar-eh?"

"Gary. I think he's been led on too. I've never even met the fucker."

"I wasn't really thinking about Marina," Baxter said. "I was thinking about her husband, his aide and the British high commissioner. We must have a conversation about where we go from here."

"I suppose."

"You have made some very serious allegations."

"You sound like you don't believe me."

"Not at all. It's just that at this stage, I do not know whether it's a police matter, or something much higher. It is beyond my experience. The bosses in London are similarly confused."

"The bosses in London are always confused."

"They have your best interests at heart, Hadley. You mustn't hate everyone and everything. It goes without saying that we are all on your side. You can be very strange. Grumpy and diffident. You go off at tangents and mix with dark and often unpleasant people. But I have not known you to be a liar."

MARINA WENT BACK to Islamabad, apparently totally cleaning up her act, according to a piece in the Daily Mail which talked about her rising from the ashes like a Phoenix and not even mentioning the Rick Astley episode. And this was the Daily Mail! There was a picture of the reporter, a handsome devil. Just Marina's cup of tea. I saw her on TV at campaign rallies, talking about relations with China, relations with India and Pakistan's resolve in fighting terrorism. Again, Rick Astley did not get a mention. I saw Marina embrace her husband affectionately. At one rally, I saw Todd standing behind her, scowling and playing with the floor with his foot. Watch out there, darling. At another, as I sat at the editing desk one evening, I saw Langhers standing behind Marina, wearing a beige cardigan across his shoulders and suffering a prolonged coughing fit as she explained, in English, how turning from Christianity to Islam had saved her life. Langhers was switching his weight back and forth from one foot to the other as though in desperate need of a pee. Or maybe he had put away one too many Sparkhayes beers.

Now I was watching Makhdoom's campaign live, from Hong Kong, enjoying being away from it all, putting some distance between us. Literally sitting back and seeing the big picture.

The TV screens went blank.

"We must apologise," the CNN anchor said. "We seem to have... um, we seem to have lost our live feed from Pakistan state television. We have been watching both Colonel Imran Makhdoom and his wife, Marina, making their last campaign pushes in separate rallies, the colonel in Lahore and his wife in the capital, Islamabad, before Saturday's election. Sorry, this is just coming in. We are hearing there has been an explosion..."

I saw her sprawling on the floor of Rick's Cafe. I saw her sitting on the beach at Shek O, patting the sand, asking me – telling me – to sit down. "Are you going to write all this down and put it in a story?" she asked. I saw her wet eyes.

"Here we go," Baxter said. "Hadley, you want to snap it? Hadley?"

"It's too vague, right? Let's wait until we have more. We don't even know if there are any casualties."

"But it's their last rally. Rallies, I mean." Baxter turned to his secretary. "I want all visuals to pull back and confirmation all safe."

"We don't even know where the explosion was," I said. "We can't snap yet. It could be a taxi running into a wall." Let it be that. A silly rabbit hutch of a taxi with a lime-green roof whose gas canister had exploded in the May sun.

"I am on to the bureau now," Fagin said, putting his hand in the air, a sign he was getting the goods. "Okay," he said into the receiver. "There's been an explosion at one of the rally sites, police say. Casualties unknown. We're snapping."

"Can we say bomb?" I asked.

"Can we say bomb?" Fagan asked. "Yes. Bomb. Lots of damage."

Show time.

I put Marina aside.

Bomb explodes at pakistan election rally site, police say, casualties unknown.

The snap was on the wire within a second of my finishing it.

"Which rally, do we know?" Fagin asked into the phone. "The colonel's. Same source? Not police. TV. Is he okay?"

Yes! You fucking beauty! Kill the fucker, I thought as I typed with renewed vigour.

Bomb explodes at usman makhdoom election rally in pakistani city of lahore, casualties unknown – police and tv.

"Hadley's snapped. You've got the TV back on?" Fagin asked the bureau. "Pictures show dozens of casualties. Dead? Definitely. Cannot say how many. State TV, right?"

PAKISTAN STATE TV SHOWS DOZENS OF CASUALTIES AT USMAN MAKHDOOM RALLY, DEAD AMONG WOUNDED.

"What's CNN saying?" Baxter asked.

"They're quoting us."

"Fantastic. Great."

"It's brilliant," I said. I really meant it. "His fucking aide wanted me to be his servant! We'll slug the urgent PAKISTAN-BOMB."

"At least fifty dead at rally," Fagin said. "Dozens wounded. The colonel's safe."

"I'm snapping," I shouted.

And so it went on. Fagin on the phone, me doing the snaps and Marcus handling the main story. It was a procedure I enjoyed much more than the reporting. It was fast, important and invigorating. Putting a story into simple words and being quoted on the BBC and CNN seconds later.

I briefly allowed my eyes to wander to another screen. A Pakistani TV station was showing an old interview with Marina. Why it would show that instead of breaking news made no sense.

"To be honest, I am not sure what you just said," the interviewer said. "You're not very specific with your policies, if you don't mind me saying so."

"You don't think there is any meaning?"

"On first hearing, I would have to say that I didn't detect any."

"You think my speeches should have meaning?" She was smiling. She was being ironic.

"Well…"

"My people love me. Already that is true. They don't listen to my speeches. I might as well go on about western pop music. They'd still come."

"With respect, I don't think so."

"But this is not England where people can have more than one opinion," Marina said. "You are for one person or you are not. If you are not, you cannot see one good thing in them or sympathise with any opinion they may have. You cannot say: 'I don't like Marina's politics, but she is right about one thing.' If you do not like my politics, there cannot be one thing that is right. That is why there is so much death. It's pure hate. Nothing in between. If you hate someone so purely, why not kill them?"

Fagin was off the phone and the bureau was now sending us the latest on the explosion in the chat room.

"Police saying it was twin blasts. Two bombs," the bureau said.

"I've got it," I said loudly.

Pakistan police say election rally site hit by two bombs

"No, Hadley. Some confusion," the bureau said. "We need to correct."

"They said twin blasts. Right, Fagin? They said twin blasts?"

"You said twin blasts," Fagin wrote in the chat room with so many typos that it was barely legible.

"Yes, twin blasts. No. Sorry," came the reply with even more typos. "There has been a second. One in Lahore and one at Marina's rally in Islamabad. Just now."

"Marina?" I said.

"I'll snap it," Fagin said. "Is Marina safe?" he asked in the chat room.

"Unknown. Many casualties."

"Is Marina safe?"

Fagin shrugged his shoulders. He crossed his fingers in my direction.

"Hadley," Baxter said. "Fagin can snap. You take a rest."

"The story has only just begun."

"Yes, but..."

"This is what I do."

"Yes, but let Fagin take over."

The chat room pinged again: "Bomb appears to have been

small drone hovering above Land Rover, police say. Marina and at least thirty others dead. Blood all over the shop. Flip-flops all over the shop. Also source to Shrubs witness. Our visuals team all safe."

"I'm on it," Fagin said. "I'm snapping."

"Are you going to write all this down and put it in a story?" I asked Fagin. He kept typing and said nothing. Baxter put a hand on my shoulder.

"CNN back on with Pakistan feed," someone said from behind me. I pushed my chair back, hands off the story. I put my hands behind my neck and watched slow-motion footage.

Journalists are trained to close their eyes, listen to a description of a street scene, picture it and retell exactly what was in their mind's eye. I was watching, observing. The closing of eyes would come later. A white Land Rover Defender, specially adapted to allow standing room in the back. Two garlands around her neck. A white shawl. Dark glasses. A crowd too close. A huge crowd. Five children leaning over a balcony above the car, one scratching her leg. One of those electricity switch boxes whose insides had been ripped to shreds. No sign of any drone. No sign of any security. No sign of anyone who cared for her. Just madmen idolising a dream. The camera zoomed out to reveal a tiny car, a Suzuki Mehran, at the edge of a sea of desperate, poor, uneducated, hopeless serfs.

"There must be a million people, Hadley," Baxter said.

Those nearest were throwing flowers. She was lively, smiling and empowered, just like she wanted the women of Pakistan to be. One security man was catching garlands and throwing them back at the people who had thrown them. Marina had to brush up on her PR, I thought. She waved to her left and waved to her right. She paused. She leant on the roof and sank her head momentarily, stood up straight and beamed.

She put down a garland she was holding on the seat behind her. She raised her arms above her head and pointed the fingers down until they were touching her veil, making the shape of a heart. "It is a gesture of affection I have for you," she had said. "A first-class gesture."

Something distracted her. She looked to the sky, keeping her arms where they were, ever so slightly arching her back. The screen went blank in a flash of yellow and orange.

"We need all this in the trunk, Fagin," Baxter said.

"Of course."

"It's colour. The hands on the head bit. It's extraordinary."

Marcus said something under his breath about a prima donna.

"What's that?" I asked.

"Nothing, Hadley."

"No, it was something."

"I was just wondering why she was standing like that. Leaning back with her arms above her head, making a heart like a ballerina."

"A prima donna, you said."

"Maybe she heard or felt something overhead," Baxter said. "The drone."

Who would have thought of it? A little helicopter-like device, a toy, hovering overhead. A dapper gadget in a country which can't even keep the electricity switched on all day and where a Goblin Teasmade is considered high-tech.

"That would be it," I said. "She heard something overhead. She felt something."

The news, of course, was hotter than red hot, and I did not have the energy to take part. Marina was hotter than red hot. Now she had been vaporised, bits of hotter than red hot shrapnel, even now, lying in her midst. Vaporised was the wrong word. I couldn't think of the right word. I just thought: what's the fucking point? Of both the blood lust of Pakistan politics and the breathlessness in the way it was reported. Fuck all the politicians. Fuck all the journalists. Fuck Fagin and Baxter and Marcus. They were all in it for themselves.

"Hadley, follow me."

Baxter brushed past me, headed for his office. I traipsed behind and sat down in front of his desk. He closed the door and took his place in his giant, black, ergonomically correct chair, his back to the harbour haze. He reached down to his bottom left drawer where I knew, from many times gone by, he kept a bottle of Black Label.

"Onward Christian bloody soldiers," I said.

"What?"

"No nothing. Just a line of Colonel Makhdoom's. I'm thankful for small mercies. The drink, I mean."

"Indeed." He quickly brought out the bottle, poured two triple shots and returned the bottle to its home. "Here we go. Cheers."

"Cheers."

Baxter swivelled a half turn, looked out over the water and swivelled back.

"Hadley, I have an idea of how you may be feeling, and I want to say that I am sorry."

"I haven't written one story."

"Never mind that now. This bombing, these bombings, must be a dreadful shock. Don't interrupt. You are bearing up extremely well, I have to say. My heart goes out to you – all of our hearts go out to you. And you must take as much time as you need before you arrive here again for work."

Was I was bearing up extremely well? Bearing up to what, exactly? If I was bearing up to anything, well or badly, it would be the first time. "Her husband did it, of course," I said.

"Well, we don't know that."

"Yes we do. The colonel and his people. That's the story we can write. I can remember her words on specific points."

"Well, we have to have a discussion. There are legal issues."

I watched a Star Ferry bobbing up and down on its way to Tsim Sha Tsui – "Sharp Sand Point" in Cantonese.

"The strange thing is, despite all her affairs with superstars from all round the world..." I didn't finish the sentence. "It's all just..." I rapped the knuckle of my forefinger on the desk. "It's just such a waste."

"It's Pakistan. It happens all the time."

I took a large gulp of the Scotch. It tasted a bit rough. As though he had filled a bottle of Black Label with Red.

"All the time," I said. "Any time, any place."

"Instead of time off, we need to get you off the desk again and on to another story. To take your mind off things. What do you say?"

"Sure. Anything."

Baxter's phone went. He listened a while.

"You realise we are very busy with the Pakistan bomb story," he said. "But yes. I'm sure we can." Baxter looked at me. "In fact, I think I may have the very person sitting right in front of me. You are looking for someone who knows the Hong Kong story well. Okay... okay. This evening. The Captain's Bar at the Mandarin. Drinks on you. Yes. Yes, you're right. The best line-up of Scotch whiskies in Asia. Very swish. I will tell him. Yes. Yes. Thank you. No, it's my pleasure."

Baxter hung up the phone, lifted his glass and said cheers again. "This man was beaten up last night for just being near the pro-democracy protests," Baxter said. "Not the first time, apparently. Said he wasn't taking part. Just an observer. Wants to give his side of the story."

"Who is it?"

"Didn't give a full name. Said China was pissed off at him for no reason."

"So he's famous, then. Who is he?"

"He'll meet you in the Captain's Bar. Seven-thirty. He says you can drink as much as you like. All you know about him is that he sounds like a prick."

"Who the fuck is it?"

"Party by the name of Kenny G."

ABOUT THE AUTHOR

NICK MACFIE was a reporter for the Sussex Express, Cambridge Evening News and Sydney Sun before moving to Hong Kong where he worked for the South China Morning Post, Agence-France Presse, Asian Wall Street Journal and Reuters. He now lives in Singapore.